BULLET

SUICIDE KINGS MC BOOK 1

NIKKI SPARXX

D1360193

Bullet
Suicide Kings MC Book 1
Nikki Sparxx

All rights reserved. Copyright © 2020 by Nikki Sparxx.
This is a work of fiction. The author holds exclusive rights to this work. Unauthorized duplication is prohibited. No part of this book can be reproduced in any form or by electronic or mechanical means including information storage and retrieval systems, without the permission in writing from the author. The only exception is by a reviewer who may quote short excerpts in a review.
For more information: www.facebook.com/NikkiSparxxAuthor
www.nikkisparxx.wordpress.com

Cover Design: Melissa Gill Designs
Editor: Jenny Sims with Editing4Indies

BULLET: SUICIDE KINGS MC PLAYLIST

"Control" by Puddle of Mudd
"Addicted" by Saving Abel
"Father Figure" by George Michael
"Closer" by Nine Inch Nails
"Move That Dope" by Future, Pharrel Williams, Pusha T
"Hurt" by Nine Inch Nails
"All Around Me" by Flyleaf
"Free Bird" by Lynyrd Skynyrd
"Sail" by AWOLNATION
"Miserable" by Lit
"Scars" by Papa Roach
"Through the Glass" by Stone Sour
"Low Life" by Future ft. The Weeknd
"Rebel Yell" by Billy Idol
"Beast-Southpaw Remix" by Rob Bailey & The Hustle Standard
"Brain Stew" by Green Day
"Sabotage" by Beastie Boys
"Heartless" by The Weeknd

PROLOGUE

Dixyn

Y ou died on a Wednesday. I felt like a piece of me died along with you. I should have come back to visit you more, and I'll have to live with that regret for the rest of my life. But even in death, you're still watching over me, giving me a way out of the hellhole I dug myself into. And I promise not to take it for granted.

CHAPTER 1

Dixyn

Never in a million years. That's what I'd always told myself about going back to Laughlin. As soon as I'd turned eighteen, I'd left that place, vowing never to return to the place where I'd been raised. However, my grandpa's funeral was an exception, and I felt like it was punishment for never visiting.

Making the four-and-a-half-hour drive alone with my thoughts after finding out my grandpa had died in a motorcycle accident made the situation worse. It gave me time to think about the bad choices I'd made since I'd left Laughlin to pursue my dreams of becoming an actress in Los Angeles.

I'd wanted to make something of myself and not just be known as the daughter of the founder of the motorcycle club, the Forsaken. I hated club life and the illicit activities my dad, brothers, and grandfather orchestrated and participated in, so as soon as I was legally able, I'd left and didn't look back. I'd basically given my family the middle finger and told them that the next time they saw me, it would be on the big screen.

What a joke that was. I'd been living in LA for a little over four years and still hadn't been given the time of day by anyone who mattered. I made ends meet as a cocktail waitress at a high-end lounge in Hollywood. I wasn't proud of it, but at least I was making it on my own ... well, for the most part.

And even though I never thought I would, I was going back to Laughlin to make a fresh start. I needed an escape from the hell my life had become, and deep down, I felt like my grandpa somehow knew I needed a reason to come home.

Tears clouded my vision as a sad smile tipped my lips. I ran my hands over the worn leather steering wheel of the 1978 Pontiac Firebird Trans Am my grandpa had gifted me on my eighteenth birthday. She was my most prized possession, and I was thankful I had the memento of him now that he was gone.

My father had property about ten miles outside the heart of Laughlin close to the California border. He owned a strip club in the casino district, which was a front for all the club's illegal dealings. Drugs, guns, you name it, and my dad was involved in it.

My dad had been in and out of jail throughout my childhood, and at one point, he'd been imprisoned for eight years. Him missing almost half my life because of the club was the main reason I resented him so much. Plus, he tried to act as though he hadn't missed the better part of my childhood, which pissed me off even more.

My mom was a junkie prostitute who'd overdosed shortly after I was born. I didn't remember her since she'd died when I was so young, and there were plenty of times I longed for a mother.

That was where the bond with my grandfather was rooted. When my mom died, he and my father took care of my brothers and me. More so my grandpa than my dad since he was always in jail or on runs. Having grandchildren made my grandpa pull back from club life, especially when my grandma was still around. They were the reason I had anything resembling a normal childhood.

Once we were old enough to take care of ourselves, my grandpa got involved with the club again. He and my dad basically ran

Laughlin during my teenage years, and my older brothers immediately acclimated to the family business. I wanted nothing to do with it from the time I was old enough to understand what was really going on. Nothing was worth going to jail or dying for in my opinion.

My dad met me outside as I pulled up to his property. His house was the only one for a few miles in each direction, which he preferred given the club's criminal activities.

He opened his arms to me with a grin as I exited my car. "Hey, Dixie girl. Long time no see."

My dad never seemed to age. He still looked the same as I remembered him from when I was a little girl, save a few gray hairs peppered through his dark hair. He was only forty-five, starting at the young age of sixteen having kids. "Hey, Dad."

We embraced, and the familiar smell of cedar and smoke washed over me. I pulled back and smiled as my father gazed over my shoulder with nostalgia. "You kept her, huh?"

I frowned at the fact that he thought I'd sell my grandfather's car. "Of course. She was Grandpa's. I'd never get rid of her."

He nodded, still staring at my cherry red Firebird. My grandpa said he'd chosen that color because of my hair. I'd been dying my dark locks bright red since I was twelve.

My dad directed his attention to me, tucking a strand behind my ear. "Your hair has gotten long," he observed.

My hair was almost down to my ass. "Yeah. I need a trim."

My dad draped an arm around my shoulder, leading me toward the house. "Your brothers are inside. The funeral is tomorrow, so we have some last-minute things to finalize before then. We could use your help."

I felt a pang in my chest as I thought about the finality of my grandfather's funeral. "Of course."

My brothers were sitting at the dining room table but sprang up when I entered. "Dixie!" My eldest brother, Jameson, greeted me, enveloping me in his arms.

I preferred Dixyn to the childish nickname, but I couldn't tell my family that. They'd just use it more than necessary to spite me, so I didn't complain.

After Jameson pulled away, my other brother Raleigh took his place, squeezing me tight enough to make me yelp. "Can't breathe," I squeaked.

Raleigh chuckled as he let go. Both my brothers looked the part of tough biker with their tattoos and muscles, and for a moment, I wished they hadn't chosen the club way of life. I didn't want them to get hurt or arrested by following in my father's footsteps. But my brothers were grown men, and I knew there was no way in hell they'd listen to their baby sister.

My dad opened the fridge as he asked, "Want something to drink?"

I shrugged. "Water is fine."

He tossed my brothers a beer, then grabbed a glass from the cabinet and filled it with water before handing it to me. I took a seat at the table, and the three men followed suit.

My chest felt tight as the silence settled over us, and the seriousness of the situation sank in. I gripped my glass, trying to avoid looking at any of my family members for fear of bursting into tears.

My dad cleared his throat. "We're planning the funeral to be at Spirit Mountain. He wanted his ashes spread there."

My grandfather was part Cherokee, and my dad and brothers took after him more than I did. I was more fair-skinned but had the dark eyes and hair of my heritage. My brothers and father had the beautiful golden skin, onyx hair, and warm brown eyes.

I swallowed the lump in my throat and nodded, my eyes burning with tears. After a few seconds, I choked back a sob, finally losing the battle with my emotions. My dad took me in his arms as I cried, murmuring calming words until my sobs settled to nothing more than a few sniffles. He might have been a dangerous criminal, but he was always there for his family, no questions asked.

And I would need that desperately in the foreseeable future.

Gently pushing away from my father, I wiped my face. Embarrassment heated my cheeks from the sudden display of weakness. I prided myself on being strong and self-sufficient, and I rarely cried, especially in front of other people. I composed myself, sitting up straight as he continued to rub my back. "Did he suffer?"

My dad's Adam's apple bobbed as he swallowed deeply. "No. He died on impact."

I nodded. My dad hadn't given me many details when he'd called me to let me know about the accident. I probably wouldn't have heard him even if he had due to the overwhelming grief that took over when he first told me. "What happens after we release his ashes?"

He leaned back, taking a swig of his beer. "I'll say a few words, then we'll do the last rev before heading back down for the wake at the Colorado Belle."

A smile curved my lips; I knew my grandpa would be pleased with the arrangements. "Sounds good."

We talked about more of the details of the funeral and wake before the interrogation about my life started. "So how's LA been treating you?" my father asked.

I shrugged. "It's not what I thought it would be, but there's definitely more going on than here."

"Any big gigs yet?" Raleigh questioned.

My failure sat in the pit of my stomach like a ball of lead. "Nothing worth mentioning. I haven't caught my big break yet."

My dad smiled affectionately. "Well, they don't know what they're missing."

I let out a humorless chuckle. "Yeah."

"How long you in town for?" Jameson asked, changing the subject.

I avoided their gazes, focusing on the water in my glass. "I was thinking about staying a while."

A smirk tipped the corner of my dad's mouth. "Stay as long as you need, Dixie girl."

"It's good to have you back around." Raleigh grinned, ruffling my hair.

I smacked his hand away with a chuckle. "Hey, I'm not a little girl anymore. I'm not afraid to kick your ass now."

My dad and brothers roared with laughter. "I'd love to see that," my dad commented.

We talked more about the plans for the following day before reminiscing about my grandpa. As the night went on, I'd almost told them everything several different times, but the words caught in my throat. I didn't want to get my family tangled up in the disastrous web of my life, but I had nowhere else to go. And my biggest fear was that my past would catch up to me—no matter how far I ran—and the people I loved would get hurt because of me.

The next morning was a blur. I made breakfast for my dad and brothers before we went to prepare the venue for my grandpa's wake. Jameson and my dad set up a large portrait of my grandpa next to his cut. After finalizing the details of the wake with the event coordinator, we went home to get ready for the funeral.

As I curled my hair, my phone rang. Matteo's name flashed on my screen, and my stomach clenched in fear. Dammit, I didn't even think about getting rid of my phone before coming home. How could I be so stupid?

I needed to get rid of my phone and fast. And I didn't want it to be traced to my dad's house, so I had to dump it somewhere else.

Rushing downstairs, I called out to my dad, "I'll be right back. I have to take care of something."

I left before anyone could protest or question me. I drove to where the Colorado River met the California border and tossed my phone in the water. I'd worry about a new one later.

Staring at the water, I sighed as a small weight lifted off my shoulders. I couldn't believe I was stupid enough to get entangled with someone like Matteo, but I'd been desperate at the time.

My shift was almost over as the devilishly handsome man walked in with his entourage. Suit tailored to fit his sculpted body, designer watch and jewelry, dark hair slicked back; he looked like the powerful boss from one of the mob movies. His dark eyes met mine as the manager approached him, then quickly ushered him to the VIP section of the lounge.

His eyes remained on me as he talked with the manager, who nodded as he glanced over at me. He waved me over, and I held my head high as I sauntered to the group, maintaining eye contact with the handsome man. I could tell he had money, and I needed as much as I could get to pay my rent the next day.

My manager introduced me. "Dixyn, this is Matteo Alvarez. Whatever he wants, you give him, you understand?"

I nodded as Matteo extended his hand, his eyes raking over me like a predator does its prey. Fear and excitement rushed through me as I placed my hand in his. "Nice to meet you, Mr. Alvarez."

"The pleasure is all mine, hermosa." He kissed the back of my hand, and heat rushed to my core. He oozed danger and confidence, and my sex clenched in appreciation.

Waving my boss away, Matteo sat down on the plush sofa and pulled me down on his lap. He twirled a lock of my hair around his finger as he smirked. "Let's get to know each other better."

. . .

9

I didn't know it at the time, but Matteo was a dangerous man. He always got what he wanted, and when he didn't, he found a way to take it by any means necessary.

At first, I was intoxicated by the power and sex appeal Matteo exuded. Men wanted to be him, women wanted to be with him, and I was the one he wanted by his side. In the beginning, I reveled in his attention; he treated me like a princess, showering me with gifts, fucking me senseless, and making sure my bills were paid.

After a few months, things changed.

Matteo snorted a line of coke off the glass table in the VIP section of the club we were in that night. He gestured to me. "Go ahead, hermosa."

I wasn't in the mood. Matteo had barely been paying attention to me, talking business all night with his men. I crossed my arms over my chest, pouting like a child in time-out. "No, thanks."

He scoffed. "No, thanks?" Slamming his drink down on the table, he stormed the few feet over to me and grabbed me by the hair, pushing my face down onto the table, right in the lines of the white drug.

"You know how hard I work for this?" he seethed, his face inches from mine. My heart pounded in fear as I struggled against his ironclad grip. "You will snort it, and you will like it."

He let go of my hair and looked at me expectantly. Everyone was watching us, but no one stepped in to help or defend me. I felt so small and insignificant, humiliated beyond belief.

"Now, hermosa," Matteo warned, his voice low and deadly. "I won't ask again."

I swallowed the lump of fear in my throat, my hands shaking as I snorted the line. My sinuses burned as I wiped the residual powder from my nose.

"Good," Matteo praised, settling back in the leather chair he'd been sitting in. "Next time, I won't be so kind, so let this be a lesson to you."

. . .

The stubborn side of me tested Matteo's "kindness" several more times after that, and each time, the consequences were more severe. A backhand to the face. His choking grip on my throat. Bruised ribs and black eyes.

Matteo made it clear who was in charge, and there was nothing I could do about it. He was the most powerful cartel drug lord in LA, and I had been foolish enough to get involved with him. I ignored the warning signs, intoxicated by his power and confidence.

Before I knew it, he was controlling and vindictive, using everything against me to get what he wanted. He'd even forced me to do some drops for him, and I felt dirty after each exchange. I'd left Laughlin to get away from that kind of lifestyle, and I ended up right back in it.

My grandfather's funeral was the perfect opportunity for me to escape. Matteo was in Mexico on some important business with some other cartel lords, so I was able to leave without his interference. I'd tried several times before to leave but was either stopped by his goons or beaten until I was physically unable to leave.

Gazing up at sky, I wrapped my arms around myself. *Thank you for watching over me, Grandpa.* I closed my eyes and sighed, overwhelmed by everything going on in my life. *I miss you so much. I'm so sorry I didn't visit. I kinda fucked up my life, but I promise I'll make it up to you.*

Tears trickled down my cheeks. I'd made a mess of my life, but I was going to get things back on track. I knew I should tell my dad, but I didn't want him to start a war with the cartel. My father and brothers were hotheaded, and I knew they would want revenge for the abuse Matteo subjected me to. Plus, I didn't want to tell them with all that was going on with my grandpa's death and their club responsibilities. They already had enough going on and didn't need my baggage on top of it.

I wiped my face and got back in my car, then drove back home to finish getting ready. I wore my nicest black dress, and my dad and brothers wore their road leathers and cuts to honor their president. With my grandpa's passing, that title now fell to my dad, who had been the VP.

I rode with my dad on his bike to the base of Spirit Mountain, where all the bikers were supposed to meet. Then, everyone who gathered would all ride up together to release my grandpa's ashes on the summit at sunset.

The Forsaken were the first club to arrive. I recognized most of the men, but there were a few faces I hadn't seen before. The guys made small talk as we waited for others to arrive.

After a few minutes, the rumble of motorcycles sounded in the distance. My dad told me that many clubs would be coming to pay their respects, even rivals, out of tradition, but the crowd I'd pictured in my mind didn't even come close to the number of bikers who showed up.

Hundreds of bikers spanned the desert before us, and my jaw dropped at the sheer number of them. "Oh, my God." I gasped, craning my neck to get a better look.

My dad sat up straighter, no doubt swelling with pride. My eyes burned with tears as I fought back the emotion of seeing so many men take the time to pay their respects to my grandfather.

My dad led the massive group of bikers up Spirit Mountain to where my grandpa's final resting place would be. As we rode, memories of my grandfather taking my brothers and me camping on Spirit Mountain flashed in my head. He would tell us stories about the petroglyphs drawn on the canyon's rock walls and about how our ancestors considered Spirit Mountain to be where creation began.

Those were the days; back before my brothers and I were corrupted by life.

When the road ended, we parked the bikes and walked the rest of the way to the summit. The whole experience was surreal; hiking up Spirit Mountain with hundreds of bikers to release my grandfather's ashes where our people were believed to be created.

Carrying my grandpa's urn, I cradled it against my chest. When we finally reached where we'd decided to lay him to rest, my father stopped and turned around. My brothers and I took places on either side of him as he addressed the gathering of fellow bikers who spread before us. "First off, I want to thank you all for coming. Some of us have our differences, but the respect for one of our own's passing is far greater than that."

A man who looked to be around my dad's age crossed his broad, tattooed arms over his chest. My first impression of him was that he resembled a fallen angel, beautiful and fierce, damaged yet perfect. I had to fight the urge to stare at him, forcing myself to focus on my dad's words.

"My father was a great founder. He was an even better man. His legacy lives on through me, through his grandchildren, through the Forsaken." He draped an arm around my shoulders. "He died doing what he loved. And he will never be forgotten."

I glanced up at my father, who nodded at the urn in my arms.

Taking a deep breath, I twisted the top of the urn and pulled it off. I'd practiced what I wanted to say the night before, but the words stuck in my throat, hindered by the finality saying them would mean.

My dad rubbed my back, urging me forward. I looked up, seeing most of the bikers with their heads bowed in respect; all except the rugged man I'd focused on earlier. His dark eyes were locked on me.

A tendril of heat coiled in my lower abdomen from his intense gaze. Averting my eyes, I cleared my throat and forced myself to speak. "My most favorite memories are of my grandfather, and I wish I had hundreds more." I looked down at the gray ashes in the urn and spoke from my heart, the words meant for him. "I know you're in a better place, and I hope you're riding the best bike for your last ride. I love you and miss you, more than the desert longs for rain."

I glanced up at my father, who nodded. I walked away from the group, going farther up the peak. "Ride well, Grandpa," I whispered, turning the urn over. My grandfather's ashes spilled out, blowing into the wind.

Tears streaked my cheeks as I watched them dance in the breeze. My brothers and father came up next to me, standing beside me for a few moments as the final remnants of my grandfather drifted away. I felt like the last good piece of me went with him.

My family led the way back to the bikes. I felt numb as everyone mounted their bikes, and my dad raised his fist in the air. "For Blackhawk!"

"For Blackhawk!" echoed all around us as the other bikers cheered in unison.

Then my dad revved his bike, starting the last rev. The sound of the other bikes joining in was almost deafening as they paid their final respects to my grandfather. They drowned out my sobs as I clutched my dad, finally overwhelmed, unable to contain the raw emotion suffocating me.

My dad grasped my arms that were wrapped tightly around him, squeezing me as he finished out the last rev. Then we led the group back down Spirit Mountain, away from my grandpa's final resting place.

By the time we arrived at the Colorado Belle for the wake, I'd composed myself. Since I was planning to stay in town, I didn't want to be perceived as weak. The weak were preyed upon by the bikers in the area, and I would never be someone's victim again.

I'd never cared for the club life, but I felt that the Forsaken was the only thing I had left of my grandpa besides my car. I wasn't about to become someone's cutslut or old lady, but I planned to be more involved.

Once everyone was settled at the wake, my father made an announcement, holding up a beer in his hand. "My father wouldn't want us wallowing around feeling sorry for him. He would want us to have the best goddamn party of our lives!"

Cheers erupted when several other bikers raised their beers, as well. My eyes scanned the crowd until they locked with the gaze of the man from earlier. The way he always seemed to be staring at me made me uncomfortable, yet enticed me. And I couldn't deny my attraction to him even though he probably had fifteen or twenty years on me.

He was a mountain of a man; at least six feet four and thick and muscular. Both of his arms were covered in ink from shoulder to fingers. The sides of his head were buzzed, but the top was long enough to pull back into a short, dark ponytail. Dark beard grazing the top of his broad chest, he looked the part of hardass biker.

And he was fine as hell.

Raleigh stepped in front of me, blocking my view. "Don't even think about it."

I furrowed my brow. "Think about what?"

He crossed his arms over his chest. "You know what. That's Ford Lawson, President of the Suicide Kings and Dad's biggest rival. So don't get any ideas—I know that look."

Rolling my eyes, I scoffed. "I'm not the same girl anymore. You don't know anything about me."

My brother narrowed his eyes at me. "Well, maybe if you visited every once in a while, we wouldn't be strangers."

Guilt twisted my stomach, and I glanced down, focusing on my shoes. "Yeah, well, I'm back now, so we'll have plenty of time to get reacquainted."

My dad draping his arm around my shoulder interrupted our conversation. He handed my brother and me a beer, then introduced me to some of the club members. I fought the urge to look back at Ford, whose eyes I could still feel burning into me.

The rest of the wake went by in a blur. I'd lost count of the number of condolences I'd been given and smiles I had to fake. I didn't see Ford again, and I was somewhat relieved. I didn't need to be fantasizing about my dad's rival at my grandfather's funeral, especially when he looked at me like he wanted to ravage my entire body.

I told myself I'd never get involved with a biker. Most slept around, cheating on their old ladies, and left on runs for days or weeks. I didn't want that kind of relationship. Then again, I wasn't looking for a relationship, so maybe sex with a hot biker wasn't such a bad idea. And the thought of pissing off my dad and brothers made me giggle a little.

I brushed the thoughts from my mind. I'd probably never see Ford again, so there was no point in thinking about him. Plus, I needed to get my life back on track, starting with finding a job. Once I started making money, I could get my own place and maybe even go to college. I didn't want to wait tables forever, and my dream of becoming an actress was out the window, so I needed a new plan.

I just hoped I didn't fuck up again.

CHAPTER 2

FORD

After paying our respects to Blackhawk, the rest of the Suicide Kings and I went back to the shop to unwind. Even though she was off-limits, I couldn't get the redhead out of my mind since I'd laid eyes on her. She was barely legal and Apache's daughter, and for some reason, that made me want her even more.

The sound of poker chips and rowdy laughter greeted me as I opened the door to the back room of my shop. I ran an auto body shop in the heart of Laughlin, and all club business was handled there.

"Deal me in." Pulling out a chair, I sat down, then fished a couple of hundred-dollar bills out and threw them down on the table.

Our treasurer, Dimes, took my money and gave me the corresponding amount in chips. I'd had our own custom chips made with the Suicide Kings club logo on them since we played regularly. I also had two custom poker tables made for our game, and the action could get pretty juicy. Not to mention it was better than going to the casino and losing money to the house.

We had two pool tables and three dartboards in the back room, plus a couple of flat screens to enjoy whatever sports were on. There was also a fridge stocked with cold beer and liquor. The crew spent most of their time in that room, so I wanted it to be as comfortable and fun as possible for my brothers.

"Did y'all see Blackhawk's granddaughter? That's a fine piece of ass if I ever saw one," Hook, our secretary, said.

I wasn't sure why, but my blood started to boil as some of the other guys chimed in their agreement. If she was off-limits for me, she was definitely off-limits for my crew. I cleared my throat, raising my voice. "That's enough! Blackhawk's ashes have barely touched the ground and y'all are talking about his granddaughter like she's a piece of meat. Have some respect."

The men were quiet for a few moments before our sergeant at arms, AK, quipped, "So she's off the table then, huh?"

I knew he was trying to break the tension, and I didn't want them knowing I had a hard-on for the young redhead, so I played it off with a chuckle. "Yeah, off the table. Ain't no bitch worth the drama."

The other guys broke out into laughter, and talk went back to the cards. Fucking Apache's daughter would definitely have consequences, and we had enough problems with the Forsaken.

So why did that make me want to do it even more? I guessed I enjoyed the thought of getting under Apache's skin.

Glancing down at my cards, I saw that I had a pair of queens, so I raised. Most of the guys folded, but I got two callers. I smirked as I darted my eyes back and forth between the two. My road captain, Kojack, and my enforcer, Dead Man. *Easy money.* Both were loose players who I could usually bet out of a pot.

The flop came out with a king of spades, queen of hearts, and ten of diamonds. I'd flopped a set, but there was a possible straight out there. I needed to bet strong to get any straight chasers out of the pot. I tossed forty bucks in as my bet.

Both men called, and the dealer turned the next card, a six of clubs. A low card like that probably didn't help either of them since they both had called my previous bet. I bet again. "Fifty."

Dead Man called my bet, but Kojack raised it. "Raise. A hundred."

All heads turned to me. I took a few seconds to think, pondering whether Kojack had better than me. The only hands that could beat me would be a set of kings or a straight, but I didn't think that was likely.

"Call," I replied, putting in the extra chips.

Dead Man folded. "I'll let you two battle it out."

The river card came out a ten of hearts, pairing the board and giving me a full house. I felt like I had the win in the bag, so I bet another hundred.

Kojack blew out a breath of frustration. "Got there, didn't you?"

I glanced up from the cards, meeting his eyes. "Bubba, I was there on the flop."

He chuckled, holding up his cards so only he could see. "Don't know how I can let this go. Damn river card."

A couple of minutes passed as he debated whether to call or fold. "Fuck it, I call."

I proudly turned over my pocket pair, and Kojack cursed as he threw his cards face up on the table. Ace Jack of spades.

A few gasps and curses sounded from around the table. Kojack had flopped a straight, and technically, I sucked out on him since he had me beat until the river card.

I shrugged as Dimes shipped me the pot. "Sorry, brother. That's the game sometimes."

He muttered, "Yeah, I know. I knew it, but I had to see it."

I chuckled as I stacked up my newly won chips. "I think we've all been there a time or two."

My VP, Cowboy, came over and leaned down to whisper in my ear. "We got a problem."

The smile from my win faded from my lips as I made eye contact with him. "Let's go to the office."

I finished stacking my chips before standing. "Deal me out."

Cowboy and I went to the office, closing the door behind us. Leaning back against the desk, I crossed my arms over my chest. "How big of a problem are we talkin'?"

My VP sighed. "The jewelers want more money for the pearls."

We spoke in code just in case anything was tapped. Getting caught dealing coke was a stupid way to end up in jail. I'd been there more times than I could count and had no desire to go back anytime soon. I frowned, starting to get pissed off. "How much more?"

"Double."

My eyebrows flew up. "Are you fucking kidding me?"

He shook his head as he slid his phone over to me. "Assholes texted me today with their new terms."

I scanned the messages, my anger rising with each word I read. "Cocky fuckers. Do they not know who we are?"

Cowboy shrugged. "Guess not. Maybe we should educate them."

A smirk curved my lips. "I think you're right." I handed him back his phone, then sat back to think out our best course of action. We needed to show them who was boss without starting a war. Tenting my fingers together, I relayed my plan to Cowboy. "Tell them it's a go. Set up the exchange. When they come, we'll show them how we really feel about their price hike, then give them our new terms."

Cowboy smiled as he typed a reply to the cartel's demands. "Done. Tomorrow at midnight."

"Good." I took out my new blade and ran my fingers along the smooth metal. "We'll see how they like my new toy."

I'd tortured and killed quite a few men, and it was as normal to me as breathing. It pretty much came with the territory if you wanted to be in an outlaw club and wasn't for the faint of heart.

We did what needed to be done for the club and each other.

People knew not to fuck with us because we weren't afraid to get our hands dirty. We didn't let anyone tell us what to do or how to do it, and we handled our shit our way.

Once we finished discussing business, I went back to playing cards, and after winning a few bills in the game, some of the guys and I decided to head to Harlot's, our bar/brothel, which was one of our more lucrative businesses. The club had revived the place when it had been failing a few years back and kept the owner from declaring bankruptcy. We provided the girls protection, and in return, we received free booze, pussy, and forty percent of the profits.

In addition to the Harlot girls, groupies typically hung around the place wanting to party with us. Several of them had been around for years, hoping to become someone's old lady. Most of them were a good fuck, and one of my favorites, Tammy, happened to be there that night.

She sauntered up to me. "Hey, Bullet. How's it going?"

I placed my hands on her hips. "Pretty good, baby. How 'bout you?"

She ran her hands up my arms, biting her bottom lip. "Better now that you're here."

I finished the beer I was drinking and smirked. "Why don't you show me how happy you are to see me?"

"Okay, just let me freshen up real quick." She winked as she walked away, but instead of going to the bathroom, she went out to the back alley.

I grinned as I followed her, my dick getting hard at the thought of being sucked.

Tammy was waiting for me as I came outside. She smiled as she approached me, then quickly unbuttoned my jeans and took my throbbing cock out.

She squatted down and took me in her mouth, taking my dick as deep as she could. I grabbed a handful of her blond locks and forced myself farther in, making her gag.

Gripping the sides of my jeans, she increased her pace, bobbing on my cock. I met her mouth with quick thrusts as I held her head steady.

"You ready for me, baby? Ready to swallow me?" I mumbled, on the brink of coming.

Tammy nodded eagerly, sucking me faster. After a few seconds, I came with a groan, still thrusting into her mouth to milk every last drop. "That's right, baby. Take my cum like a good slut."

Tammy swallowed my load as she stood, wiping her lips with a smile.

"Thanks," I said as I zipped my jeans back up and took out my smokes. I fished out my lighter and lit one up, taking a deep drag.

Tammy knew not to hang around once we were finished. I might fuck her later if she was lucky. "See ya later."

I nodded my head at her as she went back inside, leaving me to finish my cigarette in peace. My thoughts drifted to Apache's daughter, and how I'd pictured her sucking me off in Tammy's place.

I made sure to know everything about the Forsaken. Since they were our biggest rivals, we needed to know their strengths and weaknesses, and that included their family. But once the girl left for LA, we hadn't really kept tabs on her like we did Raleigh and Jameson. I couldn't even remember her fucking name.

I wondered if she was sticking around for good or if she'd just come into town for Blackhawk's funeral. I told myself that I was thinking about her because she was Apache's daughter and we needed to dig up intel on her since she was back in town, but that wasn't entirely true. She was the hottest chick I'd ever seen, with thick thighs and an ass for days, and damn if I didn't want her.

I pushed the thoughts from my mind. I had responsibilities as the president of my club. I couldn't go fucking some pretty, young thing and put my brothers at risk because I wanted to get my dick wet. There was plenty of pussy in the sea, especially when you ran a brothel.

I went back inside and got another beer, then joined the guys playing pool. We played a couple of games before the guys started breaking off to go fuck the girls.

I finished my beer, then went in search of Tammy. I needed a good fuck to get my mind off Apache's daughter, and she was always down to oblige.

I found her with my prospect, Trey, in one of the rooms. "Get lost, maggot," I boomed.

He scrambled to pull his pants up before quickly leaving the room. *Smart kid.*

Tammy smiled as I walked over to her. "I wasn't sure you'd come see me again tonight."

I pulled her to me. "Looks like it's your lucky night."

She draped her arms around my neck and kissed me. "How do you want me, baby?"

I pushed her down on the bed, trying not to think about a certain redhead as I climbed on top of her.

The next day, we had our weekly church to discuss business. Dimes went over our numbers from all our dealings, which included the shop, our drug and gun sales, Harlot's, runs, and bounty contracts.

I filled the guys in on the drop that night. We always met at an abandoned warehouse on the outskirts of town. Usually, the cartel sent four or five guys when we did our deals, and we had triple that easy, so we shouldn't have any issue in case shit went down.

"So these cunts think they can raise their prices on us. We're going to show them who's in charge."

A few grunts of agreement answered me as I continued, "We're gonna rough 'em up a bit, pay them the usual, and send them packing. If shit gets real, don't hesitate to handle business. We'll deal with the repercussions if we have to." I didn't have any problem killing cartel roaches.

My brothers all nodded, accepting the plan.

"They'll be there at midnight. Be ready and have your guard up at all times." I turned to AK. "Make sure everyone has a piece."

"Cowboy and I will handle the exchange. Don't do anything unless we do."

We arrived early to make sure we had the upper hand for what was about to go down. The cartel showed up at midnight on the dot. I recognized most of the guys from previous drops, but there were a couple of new faces.

We had a duffel bag of money open on a rusty old table we'd set up in the middle of the warehouse. The cartel thug in charge eyed the bag, then glanced up at me. "We agreed on double."

"About that," I approached, whipping my hand out to grab his throat. "I've changed my mind."

My men were on theirs like white on rice as I slammed the cartel asshole's head on the table. I took my new Bowie knife out and dragged it across his cheek. He cried out in pain as blood trickled behind the path of my blade. "You may be able to raise your prices with other clubs, but not with the Suicide Kings."

I heard the sounds of fighting behind me, but trusted that my men were handling their shit. The man beneath my blade cursed at me in a mix of Spanish and English. "You'll pay for this, *puto.*"

I chuckled, lifting him off the table, then shoved him away and pulled out my X9. Cowboy walked over with the goods and nodded at me.

"Take the money and get the fuck out of here before I change my mind about killing you," I threatened.

I kept my eyes and pistol trained on the cartel scumbag as he stared me down. "Tell your boss that the deal stays as is or we find another supplier."

After a few tense seconds, he grabbed the bag of money and headed for the exit. "*Vamanos!*"

Cowboy smirked. "Well, that went well."

I chuckled. "No one's dead. I'd say that's a win."

"The cartel will probably retaliate once they find out what happened."

I nodded. "We need to stay on our toes in case they try to pull some shit. I don't think they will, but we need to be smart."

"Agreed," Cowboy said. "We should start scoping out other suppliers."

"Good idea. This business arrangement is probably done for. Have Hook and the prospects take this back to the shop," I said, gesturing to the drugs. "I need a beer and a blow job."

Cowboy laughed. "Guess I'll see you at Harlot's"

I gave him a wave without looking back as I headed for the exit. "You know it."

CHAPTER 3

Dixyn

I spent the next week hanging out at home with my dad and brothers, and I hated to admit it, but I enjoyed their company. I'd missed them more than I'd realized.

By Monday, though, I was ready to get out of the house. I needed to get a new phone and find a job. My mind briefly wandered to Matteo as I applied my makeup. I didn't have to cover up bruises and black eyes for the first time in a long time, and I wondered if he'd figured out I was gone for good yet.

My stomach knotted as I thought about the abuse he subjected me to, and I closed my eyes. *He can't hurt you anymore.*

Exhaling a deep breath, I opened my eyes and stared at myself in the mirror. *This is a fresh start. You're free now.*

A smile curved my lips as hope blossomed in my chest. Maybe Matteo wouldn't waste his time looking for me. He had woman throwing themselves at him all the time. And even if he did find me, my dad and brothers would protect me at all costs if it came down to it, but I wanted to prevent that if possible.

I'd withdrawn all my money from my savings when I'd left LA so I had something to last me while I got settled and got basic essentials.

My first stop in town was the phone store. I had enough money to buy a new phone and set up a service plan to get me started.

Then I filled out applications to waitress at a few restaurants and bars. I didn't have much experience in other fields, but I also applied for some receptionist jobs at some of the local businesses. Desk work didn't seem like it would be that hard, and I'd take what I could get. I didn't want to live with my father longer than necessary, and to move out on my own, I needed money.

My last stop was a bar in the heart of downtown. I needed to unwind after the long day—scratch that, long week—I'd had.

Loud music and smoke filled the air as I entered. I made my way to the bar, then waved to get the attention of the bartender. She nodded at me as she finished up with the customer she was serving.

When she came over to me, she set a napkin in front of me. "What'll it be?"

I leaned over the bar so she could hear me over the music. "Scotch on the rocks."

She nodded before grabbing a glass and making my drink. After she set it down in front of me, she went to help another customer.

"Well, I'll be damned," a deep, rough voice sounded next to me.

I turned and stiffened. The person in front of me was not who I expected to see.

My dad's biggest rival—Ford Lawson.

He smirked. The small gesture made heat coil in my abdomen. "You lost, kitten? This bar, here, ain't your territory."

I arched a brow. "My territory?"

He took a seat in the barstool next to mine, then swiveled to face me. "Yeah. This bar is Suicide King territory. No Forsaken welcome."

I rolled my eyes. "I'm not Forsaken."

"Your daddy is. That makes you guilty by association."

I took a sip of my drink, annoyed by the conversation. "Look, I don't give a shit about your club politics." Locking eyes with him, I continued, "I didn't know this was your bar; I don't care that this is your bar. I've had a pretty shitty week with my grandpa dying and all, and I just needed a drink. So if you could just leave me alone, that would be fucking great."

He held my gaze for several seconds, amusement playing in his eyes before he extended a hand to me. "Ford Lawson."

I eyed him before shaking his hand. "I know who you are."

He cocked a brow, an amused smile lifting his lips. "Oh, do you now?"

I swallowed the lump in my throat. He was wearing a fitted black muscle shirt under his cut. He had several patches; one read "President" and another read "Bullet." Their logo, the suicide king from a deck of cards with motorcycle wheels behind it, sat on the opposite side. "Yeah. My brother already warned me about you."

He crossed his broad, tattooed arms over his chest with a chuckle. "They'd be pretty pissed if they found out you were here."

I shrugged, taking another sip of my drink. "I'm a grown woman. I don't answer to them."

"Well, I won't tell if you won't."

I didn't miss the hidden innuendo in his words. A thrill rushed through me at the thought of Ford being a dirty little secret.

That was a bad idea; a very, very bad idea.

I downed the rest of my drink, then got up. "Sorry for the intrusion."

As I turned to leave, Ford grabbed my arm. "Wait."

I tried to pull away, my defenses kicking in, but his grip was firm. "Let me go," I seethed, both angry and turned on at the same time. Thoughts of his rough hands running all over my body flashed in my mind.

"Didn't mean to overstep." He let go of my arm. "Let me buy you a drink to make up for my lack of manners."

"That's not necessary. Let's just forget this ever happened."

I turned to leave again, and he called out after me. "Aw, c'mon, kitten, don't you want a little taste of the forbidden? I know I do."

That stopped me in my tracks. Still, I didn't turn around, knowing how disastrous the idea was.

"Plus, it would piss your daddy off."

I couldn't help but smile.

I exhaled a weighted breath as I turned back around. That sexy smirk curved his lips, making my sex clench. I hadn't been fucked properly in months. Matteo took two seconds to get off and left me unsatisfied.

"Fine, but if you start any shit with my family, you will regret it."

He held his hands up in surrender, an amused smirk on his lips. "Ooh, the kitten has claws. Is that a threat?"

I shrugged. "Maybe."

He laughed. "Let's have a drink," he suggested, gesturing to my vacated barstool next to him. "Whatever you want is on me."

That definitely was a bad idea. But I didn't want to go home yet, and something about Ford drew me in. His roguish smile and intense eyes did things to my insides that I'd never felt before. He was forbidden, off-limits, and that made me want him even more.

One drink couldn't hurt. Right?

I sat back down. "Fine, but just one drink."

"Whatever you say, kitten." He chuckled. "What are you having?"

"Scotch on the rocks; Macallan preferably."

He cocked a brow, looking vaguely impressed. Most people thought I wanted fruity cocktails or wine, but I was a whiskey girl through and through. "What?" I asked with a huff, fighting a smile.

"I didn't take you for a whiskey drinker."

I shrugged. "Most people don't."

He smiled, then waved down the bartender and ordered our drinks. Macallan on the rocks for me, and a Maker's for himself.

He raised his glass when our drinks arrived. "To new friends."

Rolling my eyes, I clinked my glass against his, then took a long sip. I closed my eyes, savoring the rich taste. "I didn't realize how much I needed this until today."

"Yeah, I bet it's been a shitty couple of days for you."

Understatement of my life. "Yeah." I'd had trouble sleeping following the funeral. I kept having the same nightmare about my grandpa's accident. I took another drink, draining the rest and letting it burn down my throat.

"Wanna talk about it?" He signaled for another round, and even though it went against my better judgment, I didn't protest. I wanted to let loose a little, and I felt like I couldn't in front of my father and brothers. They had such high expectations of me, and I wasn't who they thought I was.

"I keep having nightmares about his accident," I replied, focusing on the ice in my glass. "Haven't been able to sleep."

He set another scotch in front of me, and I took a sip as he said, "A bittersweet way to go; killed by what you love most."

I nodded, tears clouding my vision. "The worst thing is that I didn't get to say goodbye. I left home and never came back. I wish I could hear his voice just one more time."

I wasn't sure why I was pouring my heart out to some stranger. I couldn't blame the alcohol yet, although I could feel it creeping up on me.

"We all have our regrets; some more than others," Ford stated, polishing off his drink.

"I'm sorry for being a downer." I sat up and forced a smile. I took another swig of my drink, wanting to feel anything but the sorrow trying to strangle the air from my lungs. Focusing on the burn of the scotch was better than dealing with the pain in my heart.

I smiled coyly at Ford, raising a brow in question. "Body shots?"

His already dark eyes seemed to darken more. "Are you sure that's a good idea, kitten?"

No, but I'd already decided to get wasted so I could hopefully forget about my problems for one night. I waved at the bartender, who came over. "Two tequilas with limes and salt."

She arched a brow at Ford, who nodded with a laugh. "You heard the lady."

When she came back, I grabbed the lime and put it in Ford's mouth. Then I licked his neck before shaking some salt on it. His eyes held a mischievous glint as I leaned in and licked the salt from his neck, then tossed back the shot. I winced, then took the lime from his lips with mine and sucked, holding his heated gaze.

"My turn," he practically growled. He repeated my steps, licking the sensitive skin of my neck and sending a shiver up my spine. "This isn't my first choice of placement, but we're in public."

Heat flooded my core in response to his implication. I wanted to do naughty things with Ford in private, things my dad would probably kill me for, but at the moment, I didn't care. All I cared about was that I felt something other than sadness for the first time in months.

Ford placed the lime between my lips, his eyes drawn to my mouth. I didn't have huge tits, but I did have some pretty nice lips if I did say so myself.

He took his time licking the salt from my neck. His coarse beard scratched me as he slowly trailed his tongue along the delicate skin. Then he downed his shot and stole the lime from my mouth.

I licked my lips as I watched him suck the lime. After the three scotches and that shot, I was in the blissful stage of drunkenness, feeling bubbly and happy. And with Ford so close to me, I was also extremely turned on. "I'm going to go to the ladies' room." I bit down on my lower lip, and his eyes went straight to it. "I'll be right back."

I sauntered away, casting him a glance over my shoulder that I hoped told him to follow me. Forgetting my problems for one night included getting fucked senseless.

After a few minutes of waiting in the restroom and no Ford, I touched up my makeup and tried not to let the disappointment kill my buzz. At least I could leave with some dignity still intact.

But when I exited the women's restroom, Ford was waiting for me. Arms crossed, he gave me a cocky smirk before pushing off the wall and forcing me back in the bathroom.

He locked the door behind him, then caged me between his arms against the wall, pressing his hard erection against my belly. "You feel what you've done to me, little girl?" he gruffly whispered in my ear before nibbling it.

A gasp escaped me as I tangled my hands in his hair. He didn't have the dark locks in a ponytail that night, and it fell to one side of his face. His lips crushed mine as he gripped my ass and lifted me.

I wrapped my legs around his waist as he continued to consume me. I couldn't help but moan as his tongue entered my mouth. He tasted like whiskey and sin, and I'd go to hell to get as much as I could.

Ford let me slide down his body. I was painfully aware of my need as his bulging erection rubbed against my aching sex.

Nipping at his lips, I fumbled with the button of his jeans, wanting him inside me five minutes ago.

He growled as he turned me so I was facing the bathroom sink. We made eye contact in the mirror as Ford pulled a condom from his back pocket. He never took his eyes from mine as he ripped open the wrapper with his teeth.

I tried to turn around to see his cock, but he stopped me. "Not so fast, kitten. I don't want you to take your eyes off me in that mirror, you hear me? No matter what."

I didn't think I could be turned on more, but I was. I did as he said, watching in the mirror as he put the condom on and pushed my dress up.

I felt him press against my entrance. "Remember what I said," he gruffly reminded, gripping my hips. "I want you to watch as I take you."

I whimpered with need, pushing back against him. I'd never wanted anyone as badly as I wanted Ford at that moment, and he couldn't get inside me fast enough.

His lips curved up in a sexy smirk as he pushed inside me. I closed my eyes in bliss, and he stilled. "Open your eyes," he commanded gruffly. "Watch as I fill your tight cunt with my cock."

I did as I was told, opening my eyes and focusing on his in the mirror. Ford pushed himself the rest of the way in, and I moaned in pleasure. I was full—so, so full—and it felt amazing.

Ford grabbed my hair, wrapping the long locks around his fist a couple of times before tugging my head back. I hissed from the sting, gripping the counter for support while Ford pumped in and out of me, never taking his eyes from mine as he fucked me. He was rough, and I knew I'd be sore the next day, but I didn't care. I loved the way he was fucking me.

His fingers dug into my hips as he pounded into me over and over, filling the room with the sounds of our skin slapping together and breathy moans.

"Fuck, you're so wet and tight. So fucking tight," Ford growled.

I was seconds from coming. After a few more hard thrusts, I cried out, clenching around Ford's thick shaft. I forced myself to keep my eyes on his as I shuddered with my climax.

"Good girl," Ford praised, grunting as he continued to pound relentlessly into me. Then he came with a roar, gripping my hips tightly as he stiffened behind me.

Once he caught his breath, Ford pulled out of me and tossed the condom in the trash before zipping up his pants. "I need a cigarette after that," he said, turning around to unlock the door.

I chuckled as I composed myself, straightening my dress and smoothing out my hair before following Ford out the door.

As if nothing had happened, we went back to our seats at the bar, and Ford offered me a cigarette. I was a social smoker, so I took it and put it to my lips as he sparked his lighter and lit the end. He did the same for himself, then took a long drag. "Apache will kill me if he finds out what we just did."

The corner of my lips curved up. "I won't tell if you won't," I repeated his line from earlier.

He let out a gruff laugh and took another drag of his cigarette. "What's your name, kid?"

Rolling my eyes, I let out an exasperated sigh. "I'm not a kid. And my name is Dixyn."

"Dixyn. I like that." He gave me that panty-melting smile of his. "Too bad you're Forsaken. And young enough to be my kid."

I shook my head. "How old are you anyway?"

He scoffed. "Old enough to know better."

When I arched a brow and continued to stare at him, he finally answered, "Thirty-eight."

Damn, I knew he was older, but not sixteen years older. He didn't look it. "I think I need another drink."

"You and me both, kitten." He signaled for another round. "A lot more drinks."

CHAPTER 4

FORD

I'd fucked Apache's daughter; a twenty-two-year-old kid.

And she was the best fucking lay of my life.

I didn't know what to think about that. Were my previous partners that shitty, or was the Forsaken princess just that good?

Head throbbing, I rolled over in bed, trying to shield my eyes from the light streaming through the windows.

My eyes sprang open as I felt something in my bed that shouldn't have been there. Long, red locks, fat ass, and lips to die for curled up next to me.

I'd forgotten I'd brought her home, but the night was slowly coming back to me. We'd both decided that fucking was a bad idea, but that didn't stop us from getting wasted and coming back to my place to make more bad decisions. On the table. On the kitchen counter. In the shower. Then finishing off in the bed.

A grin curved my lips. The little kitten was a tiger in the sack. She was my best one-night stand by a mile.

But now I needed to get her out of my bed and on her way.

I lightly shook her. "Hey, kid."

She stirred a little, but her eyes remained closed. I shook her a little harder. "Hey, wake up. Time to go."

Her eyes sprang open, and she sat up, then winced, bringing her fingers up to her temples. "Fuck," she groaned.

My chuckle brought her attention to me, and she jumped off the bed like it had caught fire. "Where the hell am I?"

I laughed harder at the bewildered look on her face. "My place."

"Shit!" she shrieked, grabbing her discarded clothes from the floor. "Shit, shit, shit!"

Dixyn got dressed in lightning speed before grabbing her purse. Digging through it, she cursed again when she pulled out her phone. "Fuck!"

She rushed out of my bedroom. About a minute later, she came rushing back in. "Where's my car?"

I shrugged. "I don't know. Pretty sure we rode my bike back."

She groaned in frustration. "This is not happening."

"Look, whatever meltdown you're having, can you take it outside?"

Her eyebrows flew up into her forehead. "Are you fucking kidding me? This is your fucking fault, asshole!"

I stood with a laugh. "My fault? It takes two to tango, sweetheart."

"Yeah, but you brought me here without my car and just expect me to leave without a ride?"

I scoffed. "This is the twenty-first century, kid. Get an Uber or something."

"My phone is dead." She held up the dark screen so I could see.

I crossed my arms over my chest. "Not my problem."

"Ugh! You're such a dick!" she yelled before storming out of my bedroom. I heard the front door slam a few seconds later.

I sighed before running a hand through my hair. I didn't need drama with the Forsaken, no matter how good the pussy was. It was best to rip the Band-Aid off rather than drag things out.

A few seconds passed, and the guilt gnawed at me. "Fuck," I

huffed before getting dressed and putting my cut and boots on. I was an asshole, but I didn't want the poor girl to walk in the scorching Nevada desert heat, especially with a hangover.

I went outside, expecting her to be sulking on my porch, but she was already gone. Even though I barely knew her, I'd already discovered her hardheadedness.

Hopping on my bike, I backed it down the driveway and pulled onto the street before starting it up. Then I rode toward Harlot's, hoping Dixyn had some sense of direction.

Luckily, she hadn't made it far. I pulled up next to the sidewalk. She glanced at me, then did a double take. "What the fuck do you want?"

She didn't stop walking. I followed, irritated by her bullheadedness. "You want a ride or not?"

She flipped me the bird, walking faster. "Fuck you, Ford!"

I couldn't help but laugh. She was feisty. Stubborn as all hell, but feisty. "Get on the fucking bike, kitten. It's over a hundred degrees out, and you have at least five miles to go."

Dixyn finally stopped, tapping her foot with a huff. After a few seconds, she got on the bike behind me. "I fucking hate you," she grumbled as she wrapped her arms around me to hold on.

I smirked. That wasn't the first time a woman had said that to me.

When we got back to the bar, Dixyn hopped off the bike before I'd even stopped. I chuckled as she stormed over to a cherry red 1978 Pontiac Firebird Trans Am.

That can't be her car.

When she opened the passenger door and threw her shit in before slamming it, my dick throbbed. A car like that gave me a hard-on. The fact that Dixyn drove it made her even hotter.

"That's your car?"

She stopped, looking at me incredulously. "What the fuck does it look like?"

I killed the bike and got off. I walked over, slowly appraising the beautiful piece of machinery with a whistle. Dixyn got in the driver's side and tried to start the car, but the engine wouldn't turn over.

"Oh my God, this is not happening!" she yelled as she tried to start the car again. The engine roared to life, but smoke almost immediately started billowing from under the hood before the car died.

"Shit! Shit, shit, shit!" Dixyn cursed, pounding the steering wheel with each word. "Don't do this to me. You're all I have left of him."

I didn't have to be a genius to know what she was talking about. The Firebird was Blackhawk's.

She got out of the car and threw her long hair up in a bun before popping the hood.

"Here, let me help you," I offered, approaching her.

"Don't bother. I can handle it," she spat as she went to the trunk and opened it. She came back with a dirty rag and a bottle of coolant. She shot me a glare. "You can go now. I don't want to burden you anymore."

"Look, kitten, I—"

She cut me off, seething, "Don't call me kitten."

"Fine. Dixyn," I corrected, putting emphasis on her name. "I'm a mechanic. Why don't you let me take a look?"

"I know what I'm doing." She bent over the engine, using the rag to unscrew the radiator cap. "This isn't the first time she's overheated on me. I just have to—"

She yelped in pain before cursing, pulling her hand back and cradling it with the other. "Fuck!" she hissed in pain. "Can this fucking day get any worse?"

Then she started to cry. Crying women always made me uncomfortable, and I hated it.

I placed a hand on her shoulder, trying to comfort her. "Look, I'll call one of my guys to come tow the car back to the shop, and I'll take a look at it. I'll get her all fixed up, and she'll be good as new."

Dixyn looked up at me with tear-stained cheeks. Her makeup from last night was smudged around her eyes, and she looked like hell, but she was still the most beautiful woman I'd ever laid eyes on. "I can't lose that car. She's all I have left of him."

Her bottom lip trembled, and I couldn't stop myself from running my thumb over it. A vulnerable beauty was my kryptonite. "I'll fix her, kitten. I promise."

She bit her bottom lip and nodded. "Okay."

I called Kojack to send one of the prospects with the tow truck to pick up Dixyn's car. We followed it back to the shop on my bike, and when we entered, all eyes were on us.

I knew the guys were probably wondering what the hell I was doing with Apache's daughter, and I was not in the mood. "What the fuck y'all looking at? Get back to work!"

My tone left no room for argument. The guys all went back to what they were doing, and I led Dixyn to my office. "Have a seat. I'll get to work on your car."

I closed the door as she sat down. Cowboy made his way over to me as I headed to Dixyn's car. His glare was as heated as his voice when he asked, "What the hell is Apache's daughter doing here?"

I stopped, standing tall and pushing my chest out. I didn't like to be questioned, no matter how much I respected my VP. "Are you questioning me?"

If his tone was fire, mine was ice. His Adam's apple bobbed as he swallowed, no doubt rethinking his boldness. "No, sir. But don't you think having her here is asking for trouble with the Forsaken?"

He was right, but I wouldn't admit it. "She won't be here long. I'm fixing her car, then she's gone."

I continued to Dixyn's Firebird with Cowboy following. "This her car?"

"Yeah," I answered, popping the hood.

He whistled in appreciation, just as I had. "What's a kid like her doing with a beast like that?"

"Blackhawk gave it to her."

Silence. The Forsaken were our rivals, but we respected the dead. Our beef had never been with Blackhawk, just Apache.

"So you wanna tell me what's going on with you and her?"

I bent over the engine. "Not really."

He crossed his arms over his chest. "C'mon, Bullet. I deserve to know what we're getting into."

I glared at him, keeping my voice low, but stern. "We ain't getting into anything. This has nothing to do with the club." I focused my attention back to the engine. "We'll talk later."

A few seconds passed before I heard his retreating footsteps. My head was pounding, and I needed coffee. I didn't have the patience to talk about Dixyn or the Forsaken. I just wanted to get her car fixed as quickly as possible and get her the fuck out before Apache came looking for her. I didn't need the extra drama, no matter how good the pussy.

It didn't take me long to fix the issue. When I was finished, I went back to my office to let Dixyn know her car was ready.

She stood as I entered, looking up at me expectantly.

"You're good to go. Got her all fixed up."

Her face visibly relaxed as a small smile curved her pretty lips. She exhaled a breath as her eyes briefly fluttered closed, then opened again. "Oh, thank God. Thank you so much, Ford."

Not many people called me Ford, but I liked the sound of my

name on her lips. "No problem." I handed her the keys. "Here you go."

"How much do I owe you?" She dug through her purse. "I don't have much right now, but I can pay you the rest when I get a job and—"

I held up my hand to stop her. "Don't worry about it. No charge." It was the least I could do for being such a dick to her.

Her brows furrowed. "Are you sure?"

I chuckled. "Yeah, I'm sure. Now get outta here, kitten, before your daddy comes looking for you."

She surprised me by throwing her arms around my waist and hugging me tightly. "Thank you, Ford," she whispered softly against my chest.

I couldn't help but smile as I wrapped my arms around her. Kissing the top of her head, I breathed in her sweet scent. She smelled like a vanilla cupcake. Then she left, throwing me a smile as she glanced at me over her shoulder.

Fuck, I could get in some serious trouble with her.

I shook the thoughts I was having from my mind and went to get some coffee. My brain was muddled from all the alcohol, and I needed a pick-me-up. Coffee in hand, I went outside to smoke a cigarette.

Shortly after, Cowboy joined me outside. I took a drag, chuckling. "Damn, I thought I'd have more time before the interrogation began."

He crossed his arms over his chest, waiting for me to continue.

"Fine, fine." I blew out the smoke. "I fucked her."

His eyebrows flew up, his eyes widening. "What?"

I nodded. "She was at Harlot's last night; ended up going back to my place."

His mouth was open for several seconds before he remarked,

"Holy shit." Then he frowned, narrowing his eyes at me. "What the fuck, Bullet? You want trouble with the Forsaken?"

I took another drag. "No, but they ain't going to find out. It was a one-time thing."

He scoffed. "Bullshit. I saw how you two were looking at each other. You're not done yet."

I shook my head. "I got what I wanted; got my dick wet with some young pussy, and that's it. I don't want to hear another word about it." I took another drag before dropping my cigarette and snuffing it out with my boot.

He held my gaze for several seconds before replying, "Whatever you say, boss." Then he stalked away without a backward glance.

I finished my coffee, then went to my office. The day went by pretty quickly after that since the shop was busy with work.

Close to closing time, AK came into the office. I looked up from the paperwork from that day. Dimes handled the numbers for the most part, but I liked to look over the guys' work before handing the invoices over to him. "What's up?"

"I think we found a new jeweler," he said before sitting in the seat across from me.

"That's good news. What do we know about them?"

"They're a rival of Matteo's, so they're more than willing to cut us a good deal to take away his business."

"Is the product good quality?"

AK shrugged. "Not as good as Matteo's but close."

I nodded. "Set up a meeting with them and take Trey and Deuce. Have them test it out before we make the deal."

"You got it, Pres." He stood. "You coming to Harlot's tonight?"

I was more than satisfied by Dixyn, so I wasn't in the mood. "Nah. Think I'm gonna see if some of the guys want to play some cards tonight."

"Cool. Catch you later."

My phone vibrated on the desk, the screen lighting up. It was a text from Dixyn.

Kitten: *Thank you again for fixing my car :) it really means a lot to me*

I couldn't help but smile. We'd exchanged numbers last night when she was buzzed and showing off her new phone that had no contacts in it. I'd grabbed it from her and put mine in so I could be the first.

Me: *No problem glad to help*

Kitten: *I feel really bad about not paying you for your hard work :(I'd like to repay you somehow*

I smirked. I could think of many ways she could repay me, but that would be going down a road we shouldn't go down.

Me: *I can think of some things ;)*

Kitten: *Lol maybe if you're lucky ;)*

She sent me a bunch of eggplant and taco emojis, and I couldn't help but laugh. She was going to get me in serious trouble because having a taste of her did nothing to quell my craving. I wanted more of the Forsaken princess, and I wasn't sure I could stay away.

I just hoped we both didn't end up regretting it.

CHAPTER 5

Dixyn

I wasn't ready to face my father. I knew he was going to be pissed at me for not coming home last night and would want an explanation.

I was pretty good at lying, but I couldn't think of anything that didn't involve me sleeping with someone. Even if I lied about Ford, I still didn't want to discuss my sex life with my father.

When I pulled up, he came outside. Crossing his arms over his chest, he frowned. I sighed as I turned off the car and got out. "Here we go," I muttered under my breath.

He didn't waste any time laying into me. "Where the fuck were you last night? I've been worried sick."

"I'm sorry. I got drunk and passed out in my car." I brushed past him. "I didn't mean to worry you."

He grabbed my arm, and I instinctively flinched, used to getting a backhand or a fist to the face from Matteo when he'd grabbed me like that. When my dad noticed my expression, he let go, his face furrowing in concern. "Dixie girl, what's wrong?"

"Nothing," I lied, looking away. "I just have a bad hangover and need to lie down."

My dad's face told me he didn't believe my lie as his eyes swept over me. "This discussion isn't over. We'll talk later."

"Great," I mumbled, walking away. "Looking forward to it."

I went up to my room and collapsed on my bed. I had way too much to drink the night before, and barely remembered the majority of what happened. I remembered hooking up with Ford in the bar bathroom, but everything after that was choppy at best.

I couldn't believe what a dick Ford had been that morning. Well, I guess I could. He was a biker, after all, and most were assholes. He'd made me feel like I was just a conquest, and in reality, I probably was—daughter of his biggest rival; sixteen years younger.

Then it was like he flipped a switch when my car went to shit. He went out of his way to help me when he could've just left me there.

My head hurt too much to try to figure out Ford's motives. I wasn't going to see him again anyway, so there was no point wasting my time. We both got what we wanted—a good fuck—and that's all it was going to be.

At least that's what I told myself as I drifted off to sleep.

When I woke up, my dad and brothers were gone. My mouth was dry as shit, so I went downstairs to get some water.

I rummaged through the fridge, trying to scrounge together something to eat. The men in my life didn't cook, so the fridge was pretty bare, but I found some lunch meat and cheese, and there was bread on the counter, so I decided to make a sandwich.

I sat down and winced. My pussy was still sore from the night before. A small smile tipped my lips as I thought about Ford. Even though he'd been an asshole, I couldn't deny how amazing he was in bed. And the fact he knew his way around a car was a huge turn-on.

Taking my new phone out, I started messing with it as I took a bite of my sandwich. I hadn't really had time to program anything or play with it since I'd bought it.

I furrowed my brows as I noticed that I had an unread text. No one had my number yet, so I shouldn't have any messages.

When I opened my messages app, I was shocked to see Ford's name. I didn't remember giving him my number, but as I thought back to the night before, the moment came back to me.

A smile tipped my lips. He'd wanted to be the first number in my phone and had snatched it from me before I could stop him. Then he'd entered his contact info and sent a text to himself so he'd have mine. I opened the unread text.

Ford: *Glad to pop your phone's cherry*

With a roll of my eyes, I shook my head. *Such a guy.* I wanted to text him back but had second thoughts. We should just leave things how they were before they got complicated and messy.

Then I remembered how he went out of his way to make sure my grandfather's car was fixed. Took the time to work on it himself and didn't even charge me. Not to mention, the sex was mind-blowing and drunken sex is typically anything but.

There wasn't any harm in thanking him again. Right?

Me: *Thank you again for fixing my car :) it really means a lot to me*

Only a minute or so passed before he messaged me back.

Ford: *No problem glad to help*

Me: *I feel really bad about not paying you for your hard work :(I'd like to repay you somehow*

I hoped he would get my flirty innuendo. I definitely wouldn't mind another session between the sheets with him.

Ford: *I can think of something ;)*

I giggled. My conscience made another futile attempt to tell me that continuing things with Ford was a bad idea as I paused, thinking of a reply.

I bit my bottom lip. Would it really be so bad to have some secret fun? No strings attached, no relationship bullshit, no drama; just mind-blowing sex to fulfill a need, a need every adult had.

At that moment, I didn't see the harm in it.

Me: *Lol maybe if you're lucky ;)*

After flirting back and forth a bit, I decided to download all my old apps to my new phone and use them. I hadn't been on social media since I'd left LA, but I'd made sure to block Matteo and any of our mutual acquaintances when I'd formed my escape plan, so I wasn't worried about using social media.

After linking my accounts, I logged onto my Facebook and saw I had a ton of messages from friends offering their condolences about my grandpa. One, in particular, stood out from one of my good friends from high school, Nina. I'd kept in touch with a handful of people when I'd left town, and being back made me want to reconnect.

I opened the message strand and typed a reply:

Me: *Thank you. I decided to move back and am going a little stir-crazy being cooped up with my brothers and dad. Are you busy tonight?*

A few seconds passed before she saw my message, but she instantly replied.

Nina: *Let's get together :) the girls and I were planning to go to dinner tonight if you'd like to come with.*

Back in high school, we had a tight-knit group of friends and always hung out together. The four of us were practically inseparable during our free time. I'd kept in touch with all my girls when I'd left, and I was glad I did.

Me: *Yes!! I haven't seen you guys in forever, and I need some fun in my life*

Nina: *Yay! We're meeting at D'angelo's at 8*

Me: *Ok see you then :)*

As I got ready, I reminisced about my friends. We had so much fun back in the day, and they were the hardest for me to leave behind. I was closest with Nina. She was blunt, beautiful, and always spoke her mind. She had light brown hair, green eyes, and a body most women would kill for.

Hannah was the Goody-two shoes of our group. She made straight A's, always followed the rules, and was as sharp as a tack. She was biracial, with beautiful caramel-colored skin, dark, tight curls, and hazel eyes. She reminded me of Beyonce and was just as fabulous.

Meghan was the badass of our circle. She was fearless, always took risks, and didn't take shit from anyone. She had dirty blond hair, blue eyes, and was petite. We both always joked how we wished we'd gotten more in the boob department since we were both tiny in that aspect.

Lately, more often than not, I'd regretted my decision to leave, even more so after the events of the past year. Chasing my dreams wasn't worth the pain and struggles I'd endured, especially since those dreams were left unfulfilled. Even though I couldn't change the past, I was ready to take control of my future.

Hannah and Nina were already there when I arrived. I hugged each of them tightly. "God, I've missed you guys so much."

Before they could respond, I was ambushed from behind. My other friend Meghan squeezed me, and squealed, "I can't believe you're back!"

I laughed. "You and me both. I never thought I'd come back. I always thought I'd be flying y'all out to visit me when I hit it big." I shook my head. "What a joke that was."

My friends gave me sympathetic smiles before Nina said, "None of that Debbie Downer shit. We haven't seen you in years, and we're here to catch up and have a good time."

"Damn straight," Meghan agreed.

I let out a soft laugh, thankful for my friends. "How did I make it without you guys?"

Hannah draped an arm around my shoulder and led me toward the entrance. "Hell if I know."

After we were seated and ordered our first round of drinks, I asked, "So what's new with y'all? What have I missed?"

Hannah and Meghan glanced at each other before quickly averting their eyes. I knew that look. "What?"

A small smile curved Hannah's lips as her cheeks flushed. "Well, Meghan and I are getting married."

"What?" I exclaimed, my jaw dropping in the process. Hannah was a lesbian, and Meghan was bi, but I had no idea they'd even been dating. "When did this happen?"

Both women giggled, making goo-goo eyes at each other. "We got engaged just this past weekend, but we've been dating about two years, right?" Meghan asked, looking at Hannah for confirmation.

Hannah nodded, extending her hand across the table to me to

see her ring. The princess cut diamond was stunning and fit Hannah's taste perfectly.

"Wow, that's beautiful. Looks like I've missed a lot." I felt sad that I'd missed out on such a milestone in my friends' lives. But I had the opportunity to make up for lost time now that I was back home. "I'm so happy for you guys. We have to celebrate!"

"We actually wanted to talk to you about that. We planned to have an engagement party this weekend and wanted you to come," Hannah stated, smiling brightly.

"Of course, I'll be there. I want to be as involved as possible. However you'll have me."

Meghan grinned. "Good because we also want you to be a bridesmaid in the wedding. We're planning for early next March before it gets too hot."

Excitement coursed through me. "That's great. I can't wait for all the wedding planning." I released a content sigh. "I'm so happy to be back. I missed y'all so much."

"Ditto, girl," Nina agreed. "Life wasn't the same without you, especially once these two started shacking up." She gestured to Hannah and Meghan. "It sucked being a third wheel all the time."

We all laughed as the waiter brought our drinks. I lifted my glass. "To friendship."

The girls lifted their glasses, and we clinked them together as they echoed my sentiment, "To friendship."

Following my toast, we chatted about life after I'd left. Hannah and Meghan were two years older than Nina and me, and had already established themselves more. They had just bought a house, and Hannah was a kindergarten teacher. Meghan was a nurse in the trauma unit of the hospital.

"What about you, Neens?" I asked as we ate our salads.

She shrugged. "I work at one of the casinos as a waitress.

Nothing glamorous but the tips are great, especially when the high rollers are on a hot streak."

I hadn't even thought about applying at the casinos, but it seemed like my best option. "Is your casino hiring right now? I'm looking for a job and haven't had any luck."

"We're always hiring. You should come by tomorrow and fill out an application. I'll put in a good word for you."

I smiled. Maybe things were going to start looking up. "I will. Thanks."

Our waiter exchanged our salad plates for our entrees. I looked down at my dish. My mouth practically watered at the steaming chicken and fragrant garlic butter sauce. "Oh my God, this looks amazing. I haven't had D'Angelo's in so long."

"We love it here. We were actually thinking about asking them to cater our wedding," Meghan commented.

"But nothing is set in stone yet," Hannah said. "We've barely started planning, and I want to look at other options."

"I'm sure whatever you pick will be fabulous." Hannah was very classy and elegant. She had the best taste in anything involving style, so I knew the wedding was going to be amazing.

Then Nina asked me the million-dollar question. "So how was life in LA?"

I sighed. "Not what I thought it would be. I was naïve to think I could make it out there. Almost every other person is an actor or model trying to find their big break. And you have to know someone to have a real chance."

"Well, they're missing out," Hannah said, reaching across the table and placing her hand on my arm. "You always killed it in your theater performances back in high school. If they couldn't see your talent, then they were blind."

I smiled softly at my friend. "Thank you."

"Anyone special in your life? Hook up with any hot movie stars?" Meghan asked.

I laughed. "I wish. Closest I got was a prospective actor like me. We auditioned for the same commercial, then hooked up in his car right after."

The girls giggled. "Well, at least you got something out of it," Nina joked.

For the first time in years, I felt real happiness. Even though so much time had passed since I'd seen my friends, nothing had changed. We picked up like high school had just been yesterday, and I'd never left. And I was utterly grateful to them for that. I needed them more than ever.

After we ate, we decided to get some drinks at a bar around the block. My mind drifted to the night before, and before I could stop myself, I asked, "Have y'all been to that bar, Harlot's?"

Hannah frowned, scrunching her nose. "You mean the brothel?"

I didn't know about the brothel part, but it would make sense since it was the Suicide Kings' bar; pussy and booze in one place. "I don't know. I went there when I was applying for jobs yesterday," I lied. I didn't want anyone knowing about my rendezvous with Ford. "Seemed like a cool place."

"Yeah, if you want to catch an STD," Meghan joked.

The girls and I had a few drinks before calling it a night. I made sure to pace myself so I didn't end up with another hangover the next day.

"Don't forget about the party this weekend! We're hitting up the strip club to celebrate the death of our freedom," Meghan called out after me.

I laughed as Hannah smacked her in the arm, obviously offended. "Hey, I resent that. You asked me, remember?"

Meghan pulled Hannah into a hug and kissed her. "And it was the best thing I ever did. I was just teasing."

The two proceeded to have a full-blown make-out session on the sidewalk, and to be honest, it was kind of hot.

Nina and I looked at each other and laughed. "Okay, see y'all later. Bye," I said with a wave before walking to my car.

When I got home, Jameson was smoking a cigarette on the porch. "Hey," I greeted.

He blew smoke up in the air, his eyes narrowed in suspicion. "Where were you last night?"

I rolled my eyes. "Not you, too." I was tired of the macho biker shit. "None of your business."

He blocked my path as I tried to enter the house. "My little sister is my goddamn business. Especially when word on the street is you went home with Bullet last night."

I arched a brow. "Word on the street? And who the hell is Bullet?"

"Don't play dumb, Dixyn. Ford Lawson, the guy we told you to stay away from."

"Look, I'm not a little girl anymore. I'm an adult, and I can do what and who I damn well please."

His face turned red with anger as he fumed, "So you're saying it's true?"

"No," I lied. I was still sore from hooking up with Ford so there was no ignoring that fact. But my family didn't need to know about it. Not like it was going to happen again. "You know I would never get involved with a biker. I hate the lifestyle and drama."

My brother stared me down for a few seconds, and I hoped he couldn't hear my pounding heart. "Well, let's keep it that way."

On the outside, I acted like I didn't care, but internally, I sighed with relief. I didn't want to cause a war between the two rival clubs, no matter how good the dick was. I didn't need more drama in my life.

Rolling my eyes again, I brushed passed Jameson and went

inside. Raleigh was sitting at the kitchen table, smoking a joint. He grinned at me with hazy eyes. "Want a hit?"

I sat down beside him and smiled as he handed me the joint. "Just what I needed. Thanks."

I took a long drag, holding the smoke in as I passed it back to my brother. After a few seconds, I slowly exhaled out my nose. "Damn, what is that?"

"Grape Ape. Helps me sleep."

"Does it help with nightmares?" I asked, hoping it would help me get a good night's rest.

"What are you having nightmares about?" he asked before taking a quick puff.

"Grandpa's accident."

He nodded and handed the joint back to me. "I never dream when I smoke it. Knocks me on my ass."

I chuckled. "Good. I haven't slept well in weeks."

After a few more hits, I went upstairs to bed. I planned to go to the Laughlin strip in the morning and apply at the casinos, starting with the one Nina worked at.

Just as Raleigh promised, I found a dreamless sleep easily.

That Friday, the girls and I met at Hannah and Meghan's house to get ready for the night.

"So which strip club are we going to?" I asked, applying some mascara to my lashes. "Please don't say my dad's."

The girls laughed. "We wouldn't subject you to that. We know you don't have the best relationship," Hannah said. "We're planning to go to Vogue. They have the hottest girls."

"Thank God. That wouldn't be awkward or anything," I remarked sarcastically.

"How is it living with him and your brothers again?" Nina asked.

"It's okay. Sometimes they act like I'm still a little girl and want to be all up in my business." I rolled my eyes. "But at least it's free."

"How long are you planning on staying there?" Meghan questioned.

I shrugged. "Until I get a job, I guess. Hopefully I'll get a call back soon."

Nina snapped her fingers. "Oh, that reminds me. My boss was asking all these questions about you, so I'm pretty sure she's going to give you a call."

I crossed my fingers. "I hope so."

"If you want to make some good money in the meantime, I got a waitress job at a private poker game. One of the other girls backed out, so they need another waitress if you're interested. Fat tippers," Nina said.

I needed whatever I could get. "Sure, count me in. When is it?"

"Tomorrow night. We can meet up at my place and get ready—bring your sexiest lingerie."

"Okay."

Once we finished getting ready, we went to a late dinner before heading to Vogue. I felt a little out of place going to a female strip club with my two lesbian friends, so I was glad that Nina was with us, too.

I noticed a few bikes out front, and my stomach flipped as I thought about seeing Ford again. Even though I'd told myself I'd stay away, I didn't trust myself to follow through if I actually had to be around him.

We entered and were escorted to a private VIP area. I scanned the room looking for Ford among the bikers and other patrons but didn't see him. Both relief and disappointment washed over me, and I shook the feelings away. Tonight wasn't about Ford, it was about celebrating two of my best friends.

We got settled in the plush seats as a cocktail waitress brought us a bottle of vodka and mixers. Then she prepared each of us a drink of our choice before leaving.

Then a beautiful blonde wearing a set of hot pink lingerie entered the stage. She had huge tits and an ass to die for; even I was turned on, and I was all about the dick. "Damn."

"Damn is right," Meghan agreed, licking her lips.

Hannah fanned herself. "My panties are already wet, and she hasn't even started yet."

I chuckled as the stripper sauntered toward the pole in front of us and hooked her leg around it. Smiling, she winked as she twirled on it. The woman was the epitome of sex, and she did her job very well.

I took a sip of my vodka pineapple as she continued her routine. Hannah and Meghan's eyes were glued to the stripper as Nina poured herself another drink.

I leaned over to talk to her over the music. "They should have a strip club with both men and women."

She smiled. "All-inclusive."

"Exactly. I wonder if there are any."

She sat back and took a sip. "I'm sure there are. Sounds like a gold mine."

The thought briefly passed through my mind that it would be funny if I opened up a strip club like my father. Just being competition for him would be enough motivation for me. "If it's not, we should do it."

Nina's brows furrowed. "What?"

I locked eyes with her. "We should open a male/female strip club."

She laughed as if I'd made a really funny joke, then stopped when she saw I didn't join in the laughter. "You're serious?"

I shrugged. "Why not? Neither one of us have a career or financial obligations."

"Well, one, we don't have the money to invest in something like that. Two, we don't have the education or experience to run a business. And three, do you really want to own a strip club?"

"You just said it was a gold mine. If my dad can do it, we could definitely do it."

Nina shook her head with a laugh. "Let's talk about this some other time when we're not drinking."

I clinked her glass with mine. "Deal."

After a couple more drinks and dances, I excused myself to go to the restroom. When I entered the main lounge, my eyes were immediately drawn to him like always.

Standing by the bar staring at me was none other than Ford Lawson.

Shit.

CHAPTER 6

FORD

When I went with my brothers to the strip club, I didn't expect to see my fiery phoenix. It was kinda hot seeing her there since most women didn't go to female strip clubs for fun.

As if sensing my presence, her eyes found me as soon as she stepped in the room. I smirked as I took a sip of my beer and walked toward her.

She placed a hand on her hip and cocked it when I reached her. "Are you stalking me?"

She was wearing a tight, black dress that hugged her curves in all the right ways. I arched a brow. "If I was stalking you, I wouldn't look for you in a strip club. If anything, you're stalking me."

She scoffed, rolling those pretty brown eyes of hers. "Whatever."

"What are you doing here anyway? I thought you liked dick." If the other night was any indication, she loved dick.

She laughed. "I do like dick. And not that it's any of your business, but two of my girlfriends just got engaged, and we're celebrating."

"Seriously?" I chuckled. "Well, that's fucking hot. I'd like to meet these friends of yours."

"Not in your wildest dreams." Dixyn shook her head with an

amused grin. "I'd love to stay and chat, but I need to use the ladies' room and get back to my friends."

She brushed by me, and I turned to look at that fine ass of hers. "Want me to join you?"

She flipped me the bird without a second glance, and I couldn't help but laugh. I went back over to the guys and ordered another beer.

"You're asking for trouble with that one," AK warned, gesturing toward Dixyn.

I narrowed my eyes at him. "Mind your own damn business," I growled, annoyed at everyone trying to tell me who I could and could not fuck.

AK grunted, then went back to drinking his beer. The bartender brought me another as I polished off my first one.

The guys and I found a table as Dixyn made her way to the VIP area. My dick got hard as I thought about her and her friends getting friendly behind the curtains with some big-titty stripper.

A foursome sounded really fucking great. I could show her friends what they'd been missing since they obviously hadn't been fucked right by a man.

I pushed the thoughts aside as a girl in a tight maid outfit came out onto the stage in front of us. My brothers started throwing their bills as she began her dance on the pole, but all I could think about was Dixyn and her perfect cunt wrapping around me again.

You can't have her. She's off-limits.

I took a chug of my beer as I gave myself an internal fuck you and tried to focus on the bouncing titties in front of me.

After a few more dances and beers, I had a good buzz going. The strippers had switched, and a couple were walking around the club, propositioning customers for private dances.

A busty brunette approached me, licking her lips and fluttering her lashes. The only thing she had on was a cowboy hat, silver star stickers on her nipples, a silver G-string, and boots. "Hey, cowboy," she drawled with a giggle. "Wanna have a private rodeo with me?"

I was having a serious case of blue balls from thinking about my forbidden fruit and could definitely blow off some steam. *Why the hell not?*

"Sure, sweetheart." I draped my arm over her shoulders. "Lead the way."

She led me back through the curtains that Dixyn had entered earlier. We passed by a few VIP areas, and I made eye contact with Dixyn as we went by the one she and her friends were in.

And if looks could kill, I'd be a dead man.

Smirking, I winked at her as we turned the corner into a hallway. I liked that she was pissed at seeing me with another woman. For some reason, I liked getting under her skin.

The cowgirl opened the door to a private room and led me inside. I let her suck me off, but I didn't have any desire to fuck her, so I didn't take things further. The only thing on my mind was a tiny redhead with a perfect pussy.

As I exited the room, the last thing I expected was to see Dixyn waiting in the hall. Fuming, she slapped the shit out of me, leaving a burning sting on my cheek. "Asshole," she spat before turning to walk away.

For some reason, that made me want her more. Anger and lust ripped through me as I grabbed her by the arm, stopping her.

"Fuck you, Ford!" she seethed, attempting to wrench from my grasp. "I fucking hate you!"

I pulled her to me, and she pushed against my chest. "Let me go!"

Pressing her up against the wall, I pinned both her small arms over her head with one of my hands. Her eyes heated with desire and rage as she stared up at me, tits heaving with ragged breaths.

"I don't think you want me to let you go, kitten. In fact, I think

you want just the opposite. I can practically smell your lust for me."
I leaned down, trailing my nose along her jawline to her ear as I
gruffly whispered, "I think you want my hands all over you and my
dick inside that tight, wet cunt."

Her voice was shaky as she responded, "Why would I want
anything to do with you after you hooked up with some skank
stripper?"

I smirked as I snaked my hand down to the bottom of her dress
and slipped my fingers underneath, grazing her soaked pussy
through her panties. "For the same reason I want you. You can't have
me so that makes you want me even more."

Dixyn arched against my hand as I stroked her. "I've already had
you, remember? I got what I wanted," she said breathlessly.

Chuckling, I nipped at her earlobe. "Keep telling yourself that,
kitten."

A moan left her lips. She was practically dripping on my fingers,
and I wanted to slam my dick in her perfection. I pulled back and
stared down at her, still stroking her through her thin panties. She
writhed against me, closing the small gap between our mouths as
she wrenched her arms from my grasp, fumbling with my jeans as
our tongues met.

I pushed up her dress as she took my cock out, just as eager as I
was to be inside her.

She abruptly tore her lips from mine, narrowing her eyes at me.
"You're not putting your dick in me without a condom. Especially
after you just fucked some stripper."

I chuckled, caging her between my arms. "I didn't fuck her. I just
let her suck me off."

She arched a brow in disbelief, crossing her arms over her chest.
"I don't know that."

I held up my hands in surrender. "Fine, fine." I pulled my wallet
out of my back pocket and fished out a condom. "Happy?"

"I'll be happier once your cock's inside me."

I couldn't help but smirk as I slid the condom over my hardened dick. I loved how blunt and straightforward Dixyn was, and once again, I cursed the fact that she was Forsaken. "Now, where were we?"

"Shut up and fuck me, Ford," she demanded before kissing me again.

Hooking my arm under her leg, I lifted it, then moved her panties to the side and guided myself to her slick opening.

Dixyn whimpered as I teased her with the swollen head of my throbbing cock. She pleaded against my lips, her words muffled and full of need, "Ford, please."

Even though I enjoyed teasing her, I wanted her just as bad. I slammed myself inside her with a groan, making her cry out in pleasure.

Reclaiming her mouth, I silenced another moan as I pumped my cock in and out of her. The wall shook as I fucked her against it, hard and rough, just the way I knew she liked it.

I growled against her lips, "I could get addicted to that tight cunt. I love the way you wrap around me, kitten."

Dixyn hissed in pleasure. "Fuck, it's so good. I feel like you're gonna split me open."

Neither of us cared about being out in the open in that hallway as I continued to fuck her senseless. After a few minutes, all she could do was whimper and moan my name, and I loved every second of it.

Dixyn's lips were swollen and her cheeks were flushed as she tipped her head back. "Oh God, Ford. I'm gonna come!"

I drove deeper and faster, her words fueling me. "That's right, kitten. Come all over my cock," I gritted out, on the brink of coming, too.

After a few more thrusts, Dixyn's nails dug into my shoulders, and her body shuddered against me as she loudly cried out my name.

Fuck, she was so hot. I couldn't get enough of her needy moans and juicy pussy. A couple of seconds later, I came with a groan, bracing myself against the wall as I held Dixyn up.

We both panted to regain our breath, and I brushed her fiery hair out of her face. Our eyes met as my heart continued to pound from our impromptu fuck, and a smile tipped her lips.

Damn, she's beautiful.

"What the hell, Dixyn?"

Instinctively, my stomach dropped, thinking we'd been caught by someone with the Forsaken. My body tensed, my hand traveling to my blade, preparing for a fight as we both turned our heads to the sound of the voice.

A curvy brunette stood with her arms crossed over her busty tits, but a teasing grin curved her mouth. She arched a brow. "Who is this?"

Dixyn wriggled to get out of my grasp so I pulled out of her and set her down. She adjusted her dress, trying to act innocent like my dick wasn't just inside her. "This is my friend, Ford."

"Looks like more than a friend to me," the other chick observed. "Did you two just fuck?"

Dixyn was suddenly very aware of the public place we were in, her head whipping around as she approached her friend. "Tell the whole world, why don't you?"

The girl laughed. "I think you already did."

Dixyn glanced over her shoulder at me. "See you later?"

I smirked. "Yeah, kitten."

She smiled before she turned and walked away, pulling her friend with her.

Well, that was unexpected.

I adjusted myself and zipped my jeans up, then rejoined the guys at the bar.

AK arched a brow. "Where you been?"

I grabbed a beer from the bucket in front of him. "Private rodeo with the cowgirl."

He smirked. "Oh, yeah? Did she wrangle your bull?"

"Fuck off." I chuckled before taking a swig.

I didn't see Dixyn for the rest of the night until she was leaving with her friends. As they walked out the door, she gave me a coy smile and small wave.

I couldn't help but grin. She was something else, and I wanted more of her even though I knew I was asking for trouble. I'd take as much of her as I could get.

CHAPTER 7

Dixyn

"You're not getting out of this, Dixyn. You're telling us who that sexy dad was now," Nina demanded.

After the strip club, we went to a 24-hour diner down the block to counter all the alcohol we'd consumed.

I could feel my cheeks heating as I shook my head and laughed. "Can't you just let this go one time?" I pleaded, not wanting to discuss whatever fucked-up thing I had going on with Ford. I didn't even know what the hell was going on between us, let alone how to explain it to my friends.

Hannah waggled her finger at me. "Hell no. You fucked some guy at our engagement party and expect not to tell us about it? Girl, you trippin'."

I let out an exasperated sigh as Hannah popped a fry in her mouth. "Fine, fine. But you can't tell anyone."

Meghan stuck her pinky out into the air. Hannah and Nina followed suit, linking their pinkies with Meghan's. "The pink is sacred," Meghan said, eyeing me expectantly.

I chuckled and twined my pinky with my friends', then we all pulled them back and kissed the tip. I took a sip of my water before explaining, "I first saw him at my grandpa's funeral."

"He's a biker?" Hannah gasped.

I arched a brow at her. "Are you going to let me finish?"

She gestured for me to go on, so I continued, "Then I happened to randomly walk into his club's bar one night. We had a few drinks, one thing led to another, and we hooked up in the bathroom."

"You dirty slut," Nina teased with a giggle.

"We ended up going back to his place and stayed up all night fucking." My sex clenched as I reminisced about that night. Bullet was the best I'd ever had, and instead of quenching my desire, being with him made my lust for him almost insatiable.

Hannah whistled. "You go, girl."

I snatched a fry and ate it before continuing, "Yeah, well, the next morning, he was a complete dick. Basically kicked me out on my ass like I was some hooker with no ride, a dead phone, and a raging hangover."

Meghan frowned. "Are you fucking kidding me?"

"What an asshole." Hannah smacked her tongue.

Nina leaned forward in intrigue. "So what happened?"

"I started walking back to the bar, hoping my car was still there. Luckily, I didn't walk far before he came after me. He gave me a ride back to my car, and I told him to fuck off."

The girls laughed.

"Good for you," Nina praised.

"Yeah, but then my car wouldn't start. As if the morning couldn't get any fucking worse." I let out a humorless chuckle as I thought back to that moment. "Apparently, he's a mechanic. So he took my car back to his shop and fixed it, no charge."

"That's the least he could do after how he treated you," Meghan said, crossing her arms over her chest as she sat back. She was very defensive when it came to her girls.

A smirk curved my lips. I loved the sassiness of my friends. "I didn't expect to see him again after that, but he just happened to be at the strip club tonight."

"So who is he?" Hannah asked.

I'd been hoping to avoid that question. I buried my face in my hands and sighed.

Meghan chuckled. "Damn, girl, that bad?"

I dropped my hands in my lap. "He's the president of the Suicide Kings."

Hannah raised her brows. "And that means?"

"He's my dad's biggest rival; his sworn enemy. The Suicide Kings and the Forsaken hate each other."

"Ooh, drama," Nina teased.

The girls drunkenly giggled, but I couldn't find it in me to join in. Thinking about my dad finding out about Bullet and me made my stomach knot with nerves. "It's more than that. Rivalry between motorcycle clubs are no joke. If my dad finds out about Ford, he'll hurt him, maybe even try to kill him."

Their laughter stopped, and it seemed like everyone instantly sobered. A few seconds passed before Nina tried to lighten the mood. "So the dick's that good, huh?"

I almost spit out the water I'd just drank, then coughed with laughter. After composing myself, I replied, "He's the best dick I've ever had." The smile I had fell as I contemplated the reality of my situation. "But I can't keep hooking up with him. There's no future for us, and I don't want anyone getting hurt over my lust."

Saying the words out loud made me feel emotions I didn't expect to have. He made me feel things I hadn't felt in a long time, and at an intensity I'd never experienced before. Even when we were arguing, I felt a fire inside me that had long been snuffed out by Matteo. Ford made me feel alive again.

"I think it's hot," Meghan commented.

Hannah smacked her lover's arm with a scoff. "How so? The guy could be her dad, and he could get them both killed over his selfishness."

"It takes two to tango. He's not the only one thinking selfishly," I defended. "And he's younger than my dad."

"Yeah, plus we all know Dee has daddy issues. Makes sense for her to fall for someone like Ford: older, dad's enemy, hot as hell biker," Nina pointed out.

"Hey!" I scowled, picking up a fry and throwing it at Nina. "One, I do not have daddy issues, and two, I haven't fallen for Ford."

Tossing the fry in her mouth, she arched a brow. "Yet."

I blew out an exasperated breath. "What am I going to do, you guys?"

Hannah rubbed my back, trying to comfort me. "Well, there is the obvious. You could stop seeing him," Hannah stated.

The thought of not seeing Ford again made me sadder than I wanted to admit, and there was no denying my desire for him.

"Or she could keep him as her dirty little secret," Nina countered.

"A hot, dirty little secret," Meghan added.

Hannah looked back and forth between our friends and scoffed. "I can't believe you guys. Dixyn could get hurt, and all you two can think about is dick?"

"Amazing dick," I pointed out with a dreamy sigh. Ford's cock was magical.

Hannah threw her arms out in exasperation. "You're like a bunch of children." She slid out of the booth and stormed off without a backward glance.

Meghan sighed as she scooted out of the booth. "I'll go get her."

As I watched Meghan jog after Hannah, I admitted, "She's right. I shouldn't see him anymore."

Nina shrugged. "You do you, girl. I'll always have your back."

I smiled at my friend. "Thank you."

After Hannah calmed down, we finished eating and went our separate ways. Now that I was out of my drunken stupor, I felt dirty about what I'd done with Ford. He had just hooked up with some stripper, and I'd hopped on his dick like my life depended on it. I'd made him wrap it up, but still. He had his cock in another woman minutes before me, even if I believed it was just her mouth.

I knew he'd hooked up with the stripper just to make me jealous, and it pissed me off that it worked. I shouldn't care who Ford fucked, but I did. My body was the only one I wanted his calloused hands on, and I hated that I felt that way. I shouldn't feel anything for the asshole, but apparently, my vagina was in control when it came to Ford, and she really liked him.

I went home and crashed easily. My lingering buzz combined with a full stomach helped with my normal restless sleep, and I didn't wake up the next morning until my phone rang. "Hello?" I answered groggily.

"May I speak with Dixyn Knox, please?"

"This is she," I replied, stifling a yawn as I wondered who was calling me. Not many people had my new number.

"This is Deborah Connelly with the Tropicana Casino. I wanted to see if you could come in for an interview today around three p.m."

I sat up, all traces of sleep gone as Deborah's words sank in. "Yes. I can be there at three."

I could hear the smile in her voice as she replied, "Great. I'll see you this afternoon." She gave me some details about where to meet before ending the call.

I flopped back down on the bed with a smile. I hoped that the interview meant things were looking up for me, and I finally felt like I was moving forward with my life.

I started to daydream a little. Maybe I could go back to school after I established some stability. I didn't want to wait tables forever, and I wanted to make something of my life. Journalism was my second love after acting, and I could definitely see myself working in that field. I could start at the community college in Laughlin, then transfer to a university in Henderson or Las Vegas, which were both about an hour and a half away.

My grin spread wider as I made plans for my future in my head. I'd felt lost for so long, and it was good to feel like I was getting back on track.

I sent a text to Nina.

Me: *Hey I got an interview today. Cross your fingers for me :)*

A few seconds later, she replied.

Neenz: *You got this, girl :)*

I decided to be proactive and look at classes at the community college for the fall semester. It was a few months away, so I told myself that was plenty of time to get myself together and prepare.

After I researched the English program and financial aid options, I felt even better. I could get an associate's degree in English, then transfer my credits to a university to finish out my bachelor's degree.

I couldn't help but smile.

You can do this.

My interview went so well that I was offered the job on the spot. I was ecstatic and called Nina as soon as I left the casino.

"Hello?" she answered after a couple of rings.

"I got the job!" I practically squealed.

"Are you serious? Yay!" she cheered.

I was so happy I could burst. "Yes. We need to get the girls together and celebrate!"

"Yes, girl, yes. I don't need an excuse to party."

I giggled, giddy with happiness. "Now I can finally move on with my life without Ma—" I covered my mouth, stopping myself. *Shit.*

"Without who, Dee?"

"No one. I gotta go. I'll text you later," I blurted out in a rush, anxious to get off the phone after my blunder. I didn't want to drag my friends into my past, and there was no point in talking about Matteo since he was ancient history.

A couple of seconds later, I got a text from Nina.

Neenz: *You still good for tonight?*

Shit, I'd forgotten about the waitressing gig. Even though I'd just secured a job, I needed as much money as I could get if I was going to move out on my own and go to school.

Me: *Yes, what time?*

Neenz: *Be at my place at 6*

Me: *K :)*

After confirming things with Nina, I sent a group text to the girls about the good news and planning for the celebration began.

Meghan: *Where do you want to go?*

One placed popped in my head, and it was probably the worst idea ever, but I couldn't help myself.

Harlot's.

I was asking for trouble, but I wanted to see Ford. He was always lingering in the back of my mind, and my sex ached for him constantly.

I shook the thoughts from my mind. I needed to get Ford out of my head, and the only thing I could think of was to find another man to satisfy my needs and take my mind off the forbidden biker I couldn't have.

I blew out a breath as I typed out a reply.

Me: *Surprise me.*

I went back to my house to grab my makeup and clothes for the waitress gig, then headed to Nina's.

She had a small apartment near the casino district. It was exactly the kind of place I saw myself getting whenever I moved out on my own.

I knocked on her door, and she opened it after a few seconds. "Hey," she greeted.

I smiled as I walked in. "Hey."

"You want something to drink?" Nina asked as she closed the door behind me.

"I'll take a water."

Nina grabbed a couple of bottles of water, and we went into her bedroom to get ready.

"So what can I expect tonight?" I asked as I blended my foundation.

She waved her hand flippantly. "A bunch of rich assholes who think they're God's gift to poker."

I laughed as she continued, "Sometimes they can get a little handsy, but you'll walk away with at least five hundred."

"Are you serious?"

Nina nodded. "Yep. One time, I left with a grand."

I smiled. That was the kind of money I needed. "And you didn't have to take your clothes off or do anything sexual?"

Nina finished applying her mascara. "Nope," she said, making a popping sound in place of the last syllable. "Easy money."

If I could handle asshole bikers, I could definitely handle some rich jerks.

After finishing our makeup, we styled our hair and got dressed. I didn't have much lingerie, but I did have this sexy, red, lacy corset with matching cheeky panties that bordered on being a thong.

I wondered what Ford would think if he saw me in the lingerie. I pictured him growling as he stalked over to me, heated lust in those dark eyes of his, and ripping everything off me.

My sex clenched as I thought about him. His facial hair rubbing my lips raw, his rough hands running over my skin, and his huge cock filling me over and over again.

My panties became damp with arousal, and I cursed the infuriating biker. I wished I didn't feel anything for him; that I didn't want him. But if my body was any indication, I obviously did.

Staring at myself in the mirror, I inhaled a deep breath and pushed the thoughts of Ford from my mind. *You. Can't. Have. Him.*

I'd already told myself that hundreds of times since meeting him. I knew it was wrong. I knew there was no way we could work in the world we lived in. No matter how much I didn't want to be a part of the biker lifestyle, I was forced to because I was the daughter of a club president. Everything was against us, but that didn't seem to stop us when we were together.

I sighed. If only I could get my body on board with my mind.

CHAPTER 8

FORD

The night after the strip club, Dead Man, Kojack, and I found out about a private poker game with big money on the table, so we decided to check it out. Our club game was great, but it was more fun to win money from strangers than each other.

The host was a local city councilman. We had some dirt on him, so we basically had him in our back pocket whenever we needed something, and that came in handy with some of the illegal shit we did.

I wanted to be the first to arrive so that I could scope out the other players when they came in, so we arrived about an hour early.

He answered the door, and by the look on his face, he wasn't happy to see us. "Hello, Ford."

"Johnny boy, how are you?" I greeted as I entered. "I was hurt that you didn't invite me. You know I love to play poker."

"Please call me John," he corrected, forcing a fake smile. "I'm sorry. I just figured this wasn't your scene, especially since you have your own game."

I clapped him on the shoulder, picking up on his hidden insult. We weren't good enough for his game. "Well, I'd much rather take your money than my brothers' money."

Dead Man and Kojack followed me in, chuckling.

Our host shut the door, then led us to the poker room. "Please make yourselves comfortable. The other players should arrive soon."

Before he left the room, I asked, "Is there another table?"

The irritation was clear in his strained face. "Yes, we should have two full tables tonight."

I grinned. "Perfect."

He left the room, and I took in my surroundings. He had a designer custom poker table, plush leather chairs, and a 50-inch flat screen on every wall. It was obvious the guy had money from the expensive, gaudy decor and high-end furniture.

As we waited for the other players to arrive, my brothers and I made small talk about our pretentious host. He was as stuck up as they came.

"Think he'll let me smoke in here?" I joked. The place was so clean that you could eat off the marble floor.

Kojack chuckled. "He'd probably bust that vein in his forehead."

A waitress dressed in skimpy lingerie came in, smiling flirtatiously. "Hi. Would you like something to drink or eat? We have a full bar and a caterer. Filet, potatoes gratin, and asparagus."

The guys and I looked at each other before I responded, "Hell yeah, sweetheart. I'll take a plate and a Maker's."

Dead Man and Kojack both ordered, too and the waitress left.

"You're slacking, Bullet. You never have steaks catered for our games," Kojack teased.

I shook my head with a chuckle. "I ain't a pompous asshole either."

Dead Man and Kojack laughed as John walked in with the sheriff. "Gentleman, I'm sure you know Sheriff Bailey."

"We do." We had an understanding with the sheriff; we kept our illegal business out of the public eye and did some dirty work for him, and he'd turn a blind eye to the club's unsavory dealings. I nodded at him. "Sheriff."

He tipped his hat. "Bullet. How are things at the shop?"

"Great. Business is booming."

He took a seat at the table. "Good. Glad to hear it."

Players slowly trickled in, and we were definitely out of place among them. I enjoyed making people uncomfortable and had no problem being the odd man out if it gave me the upper hand.

During the first hour of the game, I carefully observed everyone, making note of any tells or betting patterns. One of the most important factors in poker was knowing your opponents. If I knew how someone played well enough to bluff them out of a pot, the cards didn't matter.

I was playing on point and had tripled my stack after two hours. I took a break to go to the bathroom, and when I passed by the other poker room, I had to stop and do a double take.

No fucking way.

Dixyn was serving another player, wearing a lacy, red lingerie set that barely covered her ass and tits. Jealousy and rage rushed through me as the man stuck a tip in her cleavage.

I balled my fists in an attempt to control my anger. I wanted to break that motherfucker's fingers for touching her.

"Are you lost, Mr. Lawson?"

I turned to John, who was at the end of the hall. I tried to push Dixyn from my mind, but it was easier said than done when she looked like a porn star. "Just looking for the bathroom."

"Down this hall on the right." He gestured.

I forced myself not to look back at Dixyn as I walked away. "Thanks."

After using the restroom, I went outside to smoke a cigarette to calm my nerves. I didn't want to cause a scene, especially when there was money at stake.

She's just a good piece of ass. Nothing to get upset over. Keep your head in the game.

I scoffed aloud. Even I didn't believe my bullshit.

I finished my cigarette and went back inside. I'd planned to go straight back to my seat, but on the way, I ran into Dixyn in the hallway.

We stared at each other a few seconds. Dixyn's eyes were wide with disbelief before she blinked the shock away and narrowed them at me. "What the hell are you doing here, Ford?"

I couldn't help but smile. I loved that I riled her up. "I was just wondering the same thing. Are you following me again, kitten?"

She placed a hand on her hip. "I'm working. I had no idea you'd be here."

Chuckling, I raked my eyes over her. She was a dime piece and was hot as hell in that lingerie. "Why are you dressed like a prostitute?" I teased, trying to egg her on.

Scoffing, she attempted to walk past me. "I'm not doing this with you." When I wouldn't let her by, she rolled her eyes and let out an exasperated sigh. "Let me through."

I clicked my tongue at her. "You didn't say the magic word."

She tapped her foot. "Now, Ford."

I chuckled and moved out of her way. She quickly brushed past me, and I couldn't help but stare at that fine ass as she walked away.

I went back to my seat with a fucking hard-on and tried to focus on the game. But that went out the window when Dixyn walked in.

The waitresses had been rotating every thirty minutes, so I figured it was her turn to serve our table. Kojack and Dead Man both glanced at me, and I knew they remembered who she was by their stiff expressions.

The other guys were starting to get loud and rowdy from the alcohol kicking in, which was both good and bad. Good because that meant they were losing their money but bad because they were being handsy with the girls.

"Ooh, boys, we got a firecracker here now," one of the councilmen stated. "What's your name, sweetheart?"

Dixyn glanced at me before answering the man, "Dixyn."

The man grinned, his eyes heated with lust. "Beautiful name for a beautiful girl."

My blood was simmering with anger. I didn't know why I was so jealous when it came to Dixyn. She wasn't my old lady, but I didn't want anyone else to have her. Especially that pretty pink pussy.

I could tell her smile was forced when she asked, "Can I get you boys anything?"

The other players rattled off their orders, and Dixyn left the room.

"That one's a hot one," the same councilman stated. "I'd like to have a piece of that."

I stifled a growl of anger, trying to maintain my composure. Dead Man leaned over. "You cool, boss?"

I replied with a stiff nod. "I'm good."

"How much you think it would cost me to have a night with her?" the man joked.

His friends laughed as I barked, "Cash me out."

Things weren't going to end well if I stayed there. The dealer slid me a couple of empty chip racks, and I put my chips in them. Dead Man and Kojack did the same.

Dixyn came back in with drinks and served the other players. Her eyes flashed with concern as she glanced at me stacking my racks of chips.

Just get out of here before you do something stupid over some female.

I was almost in the clear, about to walk through the door with my chips when that dickhead councilman slapped Dixyn on her ass.

The next few minutes were a blur. She yelped in surprise. All rational thought left me as rage filled my veins. I dropped my chips as I wrenched the man out of his chair and pinned him against the wall with my hand on his throat.

"Why don't you keep your hands to yourself?" I snarled, trying my best not to beat him to a pulp.

Dead Man tried to pull me away. "He's not worth it, brother."

I tightened my grip as I stared down the councilman. He trembled in my grip, and his eyes were wide with fear.

"Is there a problem here, Bullet?" Sheriff Bailey asked, standing up from his seat.

My heart pounded with adrenaline, and I inhaled deeply to try to temper my rage.

"Let's go, Bullet," Kojack said, his tone a warning. The last thing we needed was to get thrown in jail over my jealousy.

I let the man go, then glanced at Kojack. "Pick up my chips and cash them in." Then I turned to Dixyn. "Let's go."

She opened her mouth to speak, probably to argue, but I stopped her by booming, "Now!"

She stormed out of the room, and I was right behind her. We didn't stop until we were outside next to my bike. Dixyn whipped around, her hair almost hitting me in the face in the process. "What the hell was that, Ford?"

I was still buzzing with adrenaline and anger. "No one touches you. No one," I gritted out.

She crossed her arms over her chest. "You're not my man or my keeper. You don't get to decide that."

Her words made me angrier. "Oh, yeah?" I stalked over to her and roughly claimed her mouth with mine, showing her who the hell she belonged to.

She kissed me back, pressing her nearly naked body against me. I groaned as my cock hardened, begging for her.

When we finally pulled apart, Dixyn's lips were swollen and red, her cheeks flushed. Her eyes were dilated with desire, and I could practically smell her lust for me. "Get on my bike now, kitten, or I'm going to fuck you on this councilman's lawn."

She did what I said, mounting my bike. Fuck, she looked so sexy in nearly nothing on the back of my Harley. Biting down on her bottom lip, she gazed at me seductively.

I'd parked on the side of the house, away from the front door and other cars. My brothers' bikes were the only other vehicles around, and if they happened to walk around the corner, they knew what to do if I was occupied.

"Fuck it," I growled, unzipping my jeans. I thought I could wait until I drove us back to my place, but I was wrong. "Bend over."

Dixyn didn't hesitate; she got off my bike and bent over the seat, displaying that juicy ass for me to see.

I smacked it as I took my dick out, then grabbed one of the cheeks and squeezed it. "Goddamn, I love this ass."

Moving her lacy panties to the side, I rubbed the head of my cock against her drenched opening. "Ready for me, baby?"

"Yes," she moaned.

I started to press into her and couldn't help but groan as her pussy greedily clenched around me. "Fuck."

My thrusts started out slow and deep, but quickly became rough and frantic. Dixyn's needy moans and cries of pleasure let me know she wanted me to fuck her exactly how I liked: hard and fast.

The sound of our skin slapping together and our groans were the only noise in the quiet night air. I pumped wildly in and out of Dixyn, desperate for as much as I could get, but never seeming to get enough.

"Oh, God, Ford, I'm gonna come," Dixyn moaned.

I slapped her ass and pounded harder, eager to make her gush all over me. "That's right, baby. That pussy is mine. Come for me."

She cried out in pleasure as I continued fucking her. A few seconds later, I pulled out, spilling my cum all over her fat ass.

Dixyn's legs trembled as she tried to stay upright in her flimsy heels. Her breathing was ragged as she glanced over her shoulder at me, giving me a wry grin. "Is this your way of marking your territory?"

Zipping up my fly, I chuckled. "I don't like people touching what's mine."

Her eyes narrowed at me. "Since when did I become your property?"

I tossed her a rag from my saddlebag, then crossed my arms over my chest. "Since I put my dick in you, sweetheart," I stated matter-of-factly.

She scoffed as she wiped my cum off her ass. "Is that so? No one told me."

"That's just the way it is in this life." I shrugged.

She tossed the dirty rag back at me. "Whatever. Unless you pay my bills, you don't have a say in who I can and can't sleep with."

I arched a brow. "Is that all it takes? I thought you'd be harder to get than that."

She rolled her eyes. "Speaking of which, you just cost me money with your little macho display in there."

The sound of throat-clearing caught my attention. Dead Man and Kojack poked their heads out from around the front of the house. "You done, Pres?"

"Have they been watching the whole time?" Dixyn asked in irritation, crossing her arms over her chest.

"Nah, just keeping a lookout." I waved them over. "You didn't want one of those stuck-up suits walking over here while I was fucking you, did you?"

She let out a sound of disgust and annoyance, muttering under her breath. I couldn't help but chuckle.

Kojack handed me a stack of bills. "That twat host gave us a hard time, but we were able to convince him to give us your share."

The guys kept their eyes on me, knowing better than to look at my woman. "Thanks, brother."

I counted out five hundred bucks and gave it to Dixyn. "For costing you money."

The frown on her face fell as her eyes widened in surprise. She tentatively reached for the money, as if afraid I was playing some kind of joke on her.

I grinned. "Take it, kitten."

She took the money, her cheeks flushing as she smiled at me. "Thank you."

The guys went to their bikes, putting on their helmets and getting ready to ride. They both got on as Dead Man asked, "See you back at the shop?"

"Yeah."

My brothers took off, and I turned to Dixyn. "Need a ride?" I smirked.

Her pretty lips curved up. "Sure."

CHAPTER 9

Dixyn

Ford ended up giving me several rides that night before taking me back to Nina's apartment in the early hours of the morning. I wasn't sure if she'd heard about what had happened, and I hoped she wasn't worried.

When Ford dropped me off, I looked at my phone for the first time since arriving at the game. I had several text messages and missed calls from Nina, so I quickly typed her a text to let her know I was okay.

Me: *Sorry for not responding sooner; had a biker problem lol I'll explain later*

I got in my car and quickly changed before driving home. I didn't need my dad or brothers interrogating me about my lack of clothing.

Luckily, no one was up and about when I got home. The sun was just starting to rise, and I was exhausted. Ford had really worn me out, but I loved the passion between us. And I wasn't about to let someone older show me up. I had to hold my own.

I washed my makeup off and brushed my teeth, then collapsed into bed.

~

My first shift was that Saturday, so the girls planned to take me out Friday night to celebrate getting a job. One of the things I loved about them was that they found every excuse to party. I needed that kind of positivity in my life.

Before I met up with them, I made a really bad decision and went to Harlot's on my way to Meghan and Hannah's. Ford and I had been texting each other here and there over the past few days. We hadn't made any plans to hook up again, but the sexual innuendos and flirtations were definitely there.

I wasn't sure what made me think that popping into his bar uninvited was a good idea, but it seemed like it at the time. It was pretty early in bar time so I wasn't sure Ford would even be there. I probably should've messaged him before showing up, but I wanted to maintain the element of surprise that surrounded our encounters.

Loud music and raucous laughter greeted me as I walked in, and my eyes scanned over the girls and other bikers until they finally fell on him.

He had some skanky, blond bimbo with fake tits in his lap. Even though I had no claim on him, anger simmered in my veins, and I clenched my fists to keep it at bay.

I should've known better after the strip club, but his jealousy at the poker game made me think that he might feel something more for me. But obviously, he didn't care about me since he had his tongue down some other bitch's throat.

I told myself to walk away, but I couldn't bring myself to turn around. I had a mean temper, which is why I'd always ended up getting the worst of Matteo's wrath since I'd fight back or provoke him.

I stalked over to them, blinded by anger, and grabbed the

groupie by her hair. She yelped as I pulled her off Ford and threw her to the ground.

Everyone turned to look at us as she scrambled to get up and lunged at me. I clocked her in the nose, sending her stumbling back in her hooker heels.

"My nose!" she cried out, hands flying to her nose, which was streaming blood. "You bitch!"

Before I could get to her again, Ford picked me up and hauled me out of the bar. I could hear all the guys laughing behind us and making catcalls before the door closed.

Ford set me down, leveling me with a furious glare. "What the hell was that? You can't just come into my bar and cause a scene like that."

My body was humming with adrenaline, and my heart pounded. "Why? You can do it with me, but I can't do it with you?" I retorted, referring to the poker game.

His eyes narrowed, and he roughly grabbed me by the jaw. "I do what I want, and no one, including you, is going to tell me otherwise." He let go of me but held my gaze. "You don't belong here. Us hooking up was a mistake. It ends now." He crossed his arms over his chest as he stared me down.

"Fuck you, Ford," I spat before turning around and storming to my car. I wanted to slap him, but my hand hurt from punching that bitch in the nose. My eyes burned with tears, but I'd be damned if I cried over that asshole.

I peeled out of the parking lot, never giving him a second glance. God, I fucking hated him.

I was able to calm myself down before I arrived at Meghan and Hannah's. I told myself that Ford was right, no matter how much it hurt. It was better to end things before they got complicated. There was no future with us, so there was no point in wasting my time, even if the sex was amazing.

I immediately felt better once I was with my girls. They'd chosen a country-western bar that had some bomb ass barbecue for our night out, and we decided to go all out with the theme. We dressed in our hottest country girl outfits, complete with cowboy boots and hats. I wore some daisy dukes and a cropped pink plaid shirt that tied at the bottom.

If Ford didn't want me, I was going to find someone who did. All I needed was a good fuck to get my mind off him.

"Are you ready to two-step?" Meghan asked, imitating a country drawl.

I laughed as I finished my makeup. "Sure thing, partner."

We decided to eat as soon as we got there to prepare us for the night. With the way we drank, it was the smartest thing to do so we wouldn't get smashed too easily.

After dinner, we went to the bar, and Hannah ordered a round of tequila. "To Dixyn," she toasted, holding up her shot glass.

We all clinked our glasses and tapped them on the bar before downing them.

Nina pointed out a table tent on the bar. "Ooh, it's ladies night. Two-dollar drinks from nine to eleven."

We all glanced at each other and grinned. "Thank God we got an Uber," I said.

We laughed as Nina waved the bartender over. She ordered us a round of lemon drops, and the bartender quickly made them.

As we downed the shot, I winced as the sour drink hit my throat. "Damn, we're going to get fucked up tonight."

The next round was a sex on the beach. We took those to a pool table nearby and decided to play a game before our next round. We definitely needed to pace ourselves if we were going to last the night.

I caught a guy at the pool table next to ours checking me out. He was good-looking, even if he wasn't as hot as Ford, and from the current selection at the saloon, he was my best option.

He was with two other guys who were also attractive, but he was the best-looking. I smiled at him as I took a sip of my drink.

He set his pool cue against the table and headed my way.

Hook, line, and sinker.

Nina was lining up the balls on the table as he reached me. He grinned, showing off a perfect set of teeth. "Hi. My name's Rhett." He extended his hand to me.

I placed my hand in his, and he pulled it to his lips to kiss the back of it. "Dixyn."

"Pretty name for an even prettier girl."

He had blond hair and hazel eyes, and was even hotter up close. I wasn't normally into the cowboy thing, but he looked damn good in tight jeans and a cowboy hat.

My stomach fluttered, but not with the same intensity as it did with Ford. I felt my cheeks heat. "Thank you."

I could feel the girls watching us as he asked, "Can I buy you a drink, Dixyn?"

I smiled. The night was going exactly as I'd wanted. "Sure. I'll have a vodka soda with lime." I decided to stay away from my usual so I didn't get trashed too fast. Plus, I kinda felt like that was a special thing I had with Ford and didn't want to share with anyone else.

Stop thinking about Ford, I mentally scolded myself.

"Comin' right up." He walked to the bar to get my drink, and the girls swooped in for the gossip.

"He's hot," Nina commented.

"Save a biker, ride a cowboy?" Meghan joked.

Rolling my eyes, I laughed. I wasn't looking for anything serious, but a girl had needs. If I was going to stay away from Ford, I needed a replacement.

Rhett returned with my drink and grinned at my friends. I introduced everyone as Rhett's buddies joined us.

"How would y'all like to play a friendly game of battle of the sexes?" one of the other guys asked.

"I'm down," Nina replied.

Hannah shrugged as Meghan said, "Sure, why not?"

I smiled up at Rhett and arched a brow. "Losers buy the next round?"

Rhett stuck out his hand with a smirk. "You're on."

The girls and I were able to throw the guys off their game by distracting them with sexual innuendos and provocative movements enough to win the first match.

As the other two guys went to get our drinks, Rhett came over to me, smirking. "Good game. I won't let you distract me so easily the next time."

I bit my bottom lip and batted my lashes at him. I played with the collar of his shirt as his eyes darted to my mouth. "Are you sure about that?"

I ran my hands down his chest, enjoying the feel of his defined muscles.

This can definitely work.

His Adam's apple bobbed as he brought his eyes back up to mine. "Oh yeah, baby. It's on."

His friends came back with a round of cinnamon whiskey. We took the shots, and I flinched as the liquor burned down my throat.

So much for not getting fucked up tonight.

The boys won the next game, so Hannah and Meghan went to buy the next round of drinks.

Rhett strutted over to me with a cocky smirk. "Told ya so, sweetheart. Your feminine wiles won't work anymore."

I cocked my hip and placed a hand on it. "We'll see about that."

When Meghan and Hannah came back with the drinks, I called the girls over to discuss our game plan. "We have to bring out the big guns, girls. This is the tie-breaking game."

Meghan nodded. "Girl-on-girl action."

I smiled. "Yep. Nina, you game?"

A mischievous grin tipped the corner of her lips. "Hell yeah. Let's show those boys who's boss."

Nina racked the balls, pushing her boobs out. Rhett's two friends were ogling her as she set up the table. Rhett cleared his throat. "Jake, your break."

Jake and the other guy were both staring at Nina's ass as she sauntered away.

Rhett lightly shoved his friend. "Dude, focus."

Jake shook his head, as if coming out of a stupor. As he bent over to line up his shot, Meghan and Hannah started making out at the opposite end of the table.

Jake took his shot, hitting the cue ball on the side and sending it into the wall of the table. It ricocheted into the cluster of balls, but only a few of them moved.

Giggling, I internally cheered at his miss. My eyes met Rhett's as he shook his head with a laugh.

I circled the table, looking for the perfect shot. As I picked the ball I wanted, I felt a large, firm body come up against me from behind.

"You want to play dirty, sweetheart?" He gruffly whispered in my ear, pressing his impressive erection against my ass. "I can play dirty."

I gasped as heat flooded me. I was liking Rhett more and more, even with Ford lingering at the back of my mind. But my forbidden biker didn't want me, so there was no point dwelling on him.

Glancing over my shoulder at Rhett, I clucked my tongue. "Excuse me, it's my turn to take a shot. Please step back."

Rhett put up his hands with a smirk and backed away. I wasn't about to let him play me at my own game, so I shook the delicious thoughts of riding him like a naughty cowgirl and focused on my shot.

I sank the nine ball, then looked up at him with a teasing grin and winked. "Guess we're stripes, girls."

I made the eleven ball next but missed the shot after that. Rhett smirked and readied for his shot, so I gestured to Nina for phase two with a subtle head nod.

Nina came over with two shots as I stood on the opposite side of the pool table from Rhett. As he leaned over to line up his play, Nina "accidentally" spilled one of the shots all over my neck and cleavage.

I gasped from the sensation, making Rhett glance up at me.

Nina set the glasses down on a nearby bar table and made a scene as she fawned over me. "I'm so sorry, Dee. I can't believe how clumsy I am."

I smiled coyly at my friend. "I guess it's a body shot now."

Nina licked her lips. "We wouldn't want it to go to waste, right?"

Our opponents were totally enraptured by our act. I pulled my hair out of the way, and Nina leaned in, trailing her tongue along my jawline. I tipped my head back, letting my eyes close as I immersed myself in our performance.

She made her way down my collarbone as I bit my bottom lip, suppressing a moan. I leaned back against the chair behind me as she reached my breasts and parted my legs so she could get closer.

I was all for the dick, but my friends and I had experimented several times back in high school. I had no problem appreciating the female form, and hooking up with a hot woman wasn't off the table.

Nina licked the tops of my breasts, then buried her face in my cleavage, making sure to get every last drop of the alcohol she'd spilled on me.

My panties were damp with arousal as Nina made her way back up my neck. I'd forgotten about our ploy when Rhett came up to us. "You win, princess."

I glanced at him as Nina continued to kiss and lick my neck, holding his gaze as I gave him a seductive smile.

"You girls wanna get outta here?" Rhett asked, cocking a brow.

Nina pulled back, darting her eyes back and forth between Rhett and me with desire. She bit her bottom lip as I nodded. "Sure."

The guys bought us another round of drinks after conceding defeat, then paid our tab, as well. Nina and I said goodbye to Hannah and Meghan as Rhett did the same with his buddies.

Rhett draped an arm around each of us and led us to his lifted Ford Raptor.

As we buckled in, he started the truck. "I'm staying at a casino nearby. That okay for you girls?"

"Yeah," I answered. I could tell by his accent that he wasn't from Laughlin. "Where are you from?"

"Dallas, Texas. My buddies and I are doing a summer road trip to California before the fall semester. Hittin' as many stops as we can along the way; Vegas, the Grand Canyon, Denver, then up the Cali coast."

Well, at least I didn't have to worry about any hookup drama since he wasn't sticking around. "A Texan, huh? Is it true that everything is bigger in Texas?"

Rhett winked at me. "You'll find out soon enough, sweetheart."

If the feel of his erection from earlier that night was any indication, things were definitely bigger in Texas.

"How long are you in town for?" Nina asked.

"A few days. I wouldn't mind you ladies keeping me company while I'm here if you'd like."

I smiled coyly. "I think that could be arranged." A few days with a hot cowboy could be just what I needed to get my mind off Ford.

Rhett pulled into one of the casino parking lots and parked his truck. We followed him inside, and he led us up to his room.

"Y'all want a drink? Got a pretty sweet minibar in here."

"Sure," Nina replied.

I shrugged. "What you got?"

"Vodka, tequila, rum, Coke, cranberry, pineapple."

"Vodka pineapple for me."

Nina raised her hand. "Rum and Coke."

Rhett smiled. "Comin' right up."

The handsome cowboy made our drinks and brought them to us. I was pretty drunk but felt amazing. By the gleeful look on Nina's face, she felt the same.

We sat down on the plush leather couch. I took a sip of my drink, then set it down on the coffee table before turning toward Rhett. I started unbuttoning his shirt, and asked, "You have a condom?"

He tucked a strand of hair behind my ear and smirked. "Of course, sweetheart."

Smiling, I leaned in to kiss him, slipping my hands under his unbuttoned shirt across the smooth skin of his defined chest.

Nina went to work unzipping his jeans, then pulled his cock out. She leaned over and started sucking, which made Rhett gasp against my mouth. I bit down on his bottom lip before he roughly recaptured my lips, kissing me until I was breathless.

His fingers feathered up my thighs, under my shorts, slipping beneath my damp panties. He stuck two fingers inside me as he growled, "God, you're so wet."

He fingered me as Nina sucked him off. When she finished, she stood, pulling me up with her before leading me to the bed.

Rhett watched us as we undressed each other. Nina was gorgeous, especially with flushed cheeks and swollen lips. She had curves in all the right places and perfect olive skin. Not many women turned me on, but Nina was one of the few who did.

"You coming, cowboy?" I asked as Nina took my nipple in her mouth, both of us completely naked. I played with her breasts as I gave Rhett a playful wink.

He practically jumped off the couch, removing his shirt as he made his way over to us. I giggled at his enthusiasm as he fished his wallet from his back pocket and took out a condom, then rushed to kick his jeans off.

He slipped the condom over his cock, which was already hard again before climbing on the bed with us.

Nina laid me down, making her way down my body until she was at my sex. She moaned as she licked me from my opening to my sensitive bud, then teased it with her tongue.

I bit my bottom lip, playing with my nipple as I made eye contact with Rhett. Nina was bent over me, ass up, and Rhett positioned himself behind her.

She gasped against my sex as Rhett thrust himself into her, his eyes still locked on mine. Gripping her hips, he began to pound into Nina as she sucked and nipped my sex.

We were both writhing and whimpering within seconds, on the cusp of coming. We'd had a couple of threesomes during our senior year of high school, but none were this hot. High school boys had nothing on the rugged cowboy.

Rhett didn't show any signs of slowing down, and I hoped he was saving some for me. I definitely wanted a taste of him, especially his Texas-sized cock.

I cried out as Nina flicked my clit in the perfect spot, shuddering with my climax. A few seconds later, she did the same, knotting her fingers in the sheets on either side of me as she groaned in pleasure.

She collapsed on the bed next to me, panting heavily. Her eyelids fluttered closed as a satisfied smile crept over her lips.

I turned my attention to Rhett. His chiseled body was slick with sweat, which made him even hotter to me.

Holding my gaze, he crawled over to me, leaning down between my legs. "I've been thinking about tasting you all night, sweetheart." He kissed the inside of my thigh, then nipped the same spot before running his fingers over my drenched sex. "And that pretty pussy is all juicy and ready for me."

He started slowly at first, licking and kissing my sex reverently, but soon became more rough and frantic as though he couldn't get enough. I moaned with need as he devoured my sex, nipping and teasing my clit with his teeth and tongue. "Oh, God, I'm gonna come."

He abruptly pulled away, and I whimpered from the loss of his mouth. "The only way you're coming is on my cock," Rhett informed, smirking down at me. He positioned himself at my entrance, teasing me with the head of his swollen member. "Ready for me, baby?"

"Yes," I murmured, tipping my head back as I waited for him to enter me. Ford flashed in my head, and I tried to push the thought of him away. A few torturous seconds later, I felt Rhett stretching my walls, and I couldn't help but moan as he completely filled me.

Even though he wasn't as big as Ford, he was still impressive. His hands weren't as rough and neither were his thrusts, but they'd get the job done.

I closed my eyes, trying to focus on the blissful sensations, but all I saw was Ford behind my closed lids. I wanted him even while I was being fucked by another man. After having him inside me, being with someone else didn't feel the same, as if something was missing.

Damn infuriating biker.

Nina stirred next to me, propping herself up on her elbow. Desire coated her face as she bit her bottom lip, watching Rhett fuck me.

He pounded into me, and after a few minutes, he let out a guttural groan as he came. I, on the other hand, was unable to come because I couldn't stop thinking about what I was missing with Ford.

As Rhett collapsed next to me, Nina climbed over me onto him. "My turn," she said, leaning down to kiss him. She began to stroke him, attempting to get him hard again.

After Nina accomplished her task, their moans filled the air as she mounted him, slowly riding his cock. They were completely focused on each other, and as they fucked, I couldn't help but worry that Ford had ruined me for anyone else.

CHAPTER 10

FORD

"Some of the prospects saw a few of Matteo's men in town," Dead Man informed me at our weekly church.

I nodded. I'd expected him to send scouts after the message I'd given. "Have Trey and Deuce tail 'em. I want to know who they're talking to and what they're doing. If they take a shit, I want to know about it." We needed to be prepared in case they wanted a war.

Dead Man chuckled with a nod. "You got it, Pres."

"Good news is we found another jeweler. The prospects tested the merchandise and approve." Everyone glanced at Trey and Deuce, and they both gave two thumbs up. The guys let out a collective chuckle. "Plus, they're giving us a hell of a good deal. We have an exchange set up for this weekend. AK, I want you to dig up all you can on them before we get into bed with them."

"On it, boss."

After discussing a few more minor issues, I concluded church. Dead Man pulled me aside as everyone else went separate ways. "Can I talk to you in private?"

My brows furrowed as I wondered what he wanted to talk about since we'd just finalized our business. "Yeah, let's step into the office."

Once we were behind closed doors, I leaned back against my desk. "Speak freely, brother."

"One of the prospects mentioned that they heard the cartel scouts asking about a redhead from LA."

My blood started to boil, and I clenched my fists, trying to keep my anger at bay. The thought of them touching Dixyn made my gut tense. "What?" I gritted out.

"They weren't able to hear more without being made, but I thought you might want to know."

My mind started running a mile a minute, trying to figure out what the cartel wanted with Dixyn. I hadn't heard of Apache making any bad deals, and we knew everything that the Forsaken were up to. "Have Trey confirm that it's her and find out what they want with her."

Dead Man nodded. "Sure thing, boss."

He turned to open the door, but I stopped him. "And Dead Man?"

He looked back at me. "Yeah, boss?"

"Don't tell anyone else about this. Just you, me, and that prospect."

He nodded. "Okay."

An urge to find Dixyn overcame me. Even though I'd ended things a couple of weeks back, I hadn't stopped thinking about her. I'd fucked a few other chicks, but all I could think about when I was inside them was her. They didn't feel as good and it took me twice as long to get off.

Not only did I want to see her and feel that tight cunt wrapped around me, but I suddenly had this instinctive need to protect her. The thought of any cartel scum putting their hands on her made rage simmer through me. If they touched one hair on her pretty head, I was going to rain down hell on them.

We kept tabs on all the Forsaken, and now that included Dixyn.

We had phone numbers, addresses, frequent hangouts, and known associates. We didn't have much on Dixyn since she'd just moved back, but I knew she'd just gotten a job at one of the casinos. I planned to pay her a visit to make sure she was okay.

I decided to hit the casino solo so I didn't have to hear any shit from the guys. Cowboy, Dead Man, Kojack, and AK knew something was going on between Dixyn and me, and I didn't want them asking questions.

I entered the building and headed for the main floor, hoping I'd be able to find her quickly. It was during the day on a Sunday, so it wasn't too packed, but the casino was huge. And with all the machines and tables, it wasn't the easiest to pick people out.

I decided to sit at a slot machine in the center of the main floor and see if I could spot her. If we were both on the move, it would be more difficult to find her, and I didn't want to be at the casino all day.

Several minutes passed and a few waitresses passed by, but no sign of my redhead.

I took out a cigarette and lit it before taking a long drag to temper my impatience.

"You looking for Dee?"

The voice sounded familiar, so I turned to place it. Standing a few feet away was Dixyn's friend from the strip club. "Yeah. You work here too?"

She smiled. "Got her the job."

I wasn't one for small talk. I took another drag of my cigarette. "You know where she is?"

The pretty brunette pursed her lips to the side in thought. "I think her section is over by the roulette and craps tables today."

Standing, I took one last puff before putting out my cigarette. "Thanks." I headed toward the table games, hoping Dixyn's friend was right.

Once I found the craps tables, I stopped and looked around, searching for my beauty. I finally picked out her bright red hair at one of the roulette tables a few tables away.

I made my way over to her. She smiled warmly at a player as she handed him a drink, and he tipped her some chips.

When she saw me, her demeanor completely shifted. Narrowing her eyes, she stalked over to me. "What the hell are you doing here?" she asked, her voice an angry whisper.

"Nice to see you, too, kitten." I chuckled.

"Well, the last time I saw you, you told me to get lost. So I'm confused as to why you're here."

"Look, about that ... Can we talk?"

She frowned, darting her eyes around. "I'm working. I can't just drop everything to talk to you. I need to get back to the players."

"Wait," I said, stopping her. Dixyn looked at me impatiently as I stepped over to the nearest roulette table and took out a hundred-dollar bill. "Pick a number," I said as the attendant spun the ball onto the roulette wheel.

Her eyebrows furrowed in confusion. "What?"

"If I have to play to get you to talk to me, I have no problem doing so. So pick a number."

Dixyn's wide, dark eyes darted between the wheel and the table several times, but she still didn't respond.

"Now, kitten."

The wheel started to slow as she blurted out, "Nine."

I slammed my money down on the nine right before the attendant announced no more bets.

I smirked at Dixyn as she gaped at me. "That wasn't so hard now was it?"

"You just put a hundred dollars on my number," she stammered, flustered. "What if you lose that because of me?"

I shrugged, amused by her reaction. I loved seeing her all worked up.

As she was about to speak again, the attendant called out, "Nine!"

Dixyn's eyes widened in surprise as I took a glance at the wheel. Sure enough, the ball had landed on the nine.

"Oh my God," Dixyn murmured in surprise.

I was shocked for a few moments myself before I cheered out, "Yeah!" I grinned widely at Dixyn. "You just won me thirty-five hundred bucks, kitten."

Her lips curved into a huge smile, and she let out a little squeal of delight.

As the attendant called a pit boss and stacked my payout, I asked, "When you get off? I'm taking you out to celebrate."

Her cheeks flushed. "I get off at eight."

"All right. I'll pick you up at eight."

"Okay." Dixyn gave me a small wave before returning to serve customers. I left after getting my money and went back to the shop. I felt a hundred times better after seeing her alive and well, and winning thirty-five hundred dollars was just icing on the cake.

When eight o'clock rolled around, I pulled up outside the casino on my bike. Dixyn came out a few minutes later, dressed in some tight jeans and a white halter top. She looked fine as hell, exactly what I wanted sitting on the back of my bike.

She approached me with a smile. "Good thing I brought a change of clothes."

I handed her a helmet. "Ready?"

She hesitated. "You think this is a good idea? Being seen together?"

I shrugged. "Helmet should cover most of your face."

"Whatever you say." She laughed before pulling the helmet over her head.

I patted the seat behind me. "Hop on."

She jumped on and secured her arms around my waist.

"Hang on tight, kitten." I revved my bike and pulled out of the parking lot, turning on the main street.

"Where are we going?" Dixyn yelled over the roar of my engine.

"You'll see," I yelled back.

I had decided to take Dixyn to my favorite place, the Black Bear Diner. It wasn't fancy but had the best comfort food. Plus, we wouldn't have to worry about running into anyone we knew since it was in Bullhead City, not Laughlin.

I pulled up outside and put my bike in park. Dixyn hopped off the back and slipped her helmet off. "I've never been here before."

I took my helmet off and took hers from her, then put them in my saddlebag. "Well, you're in for a treat, then. This is my favorite spot."

Opening the door for her, I followed her inside. We were seated in a booth near the back, and Dixyn looked around, taking in all the décor. "This place sure is homey."

"Yeah. Food is, too."

A waitress in a plaid lumberjack shirt came to take our drink order.

Dixyn opened the menu and scanned the pages. She glanced up at me with a wry grin. "Let me guess, you like the Bigfoot Chicken Fried Steak?"

I chuckled. "What can I say? I'm a big guy."

She playfully rolled her eyes and went back to looking at the menu. "I think I'll have the potpie. Or maybe the pot roast."

I smiled. I liked a girl who wasn't afraid to eat. "Both are great."

She set her menu down. "Have you had everything here?"

"Just about. Minus the pasta and girly shit."

Dixyn laughed as the waitress came back with our drinks. We

ordered our food, and I took a drink of my Arnold Palmer. "The only bad thing about this place is they don't have booze."

She laughed again. "Well, I assume this celebration will include booze."

"Of course. And a tattoo."

Her brows furrowed. "A tattoo?"

"Yeah. I always get a tattoo to celebrate something; that way they all have meaning."

She played with her straw, smiling at me. "That's really cool."

"You got any ink?" I asked. I hadn't noticed any when I'd fucked her, but I hadn't been looking.

She shook her head. "I've always wanted to, but never have because it's not the most desirable for actresses."

I nodded in understanding. "What about now?"

She shrugged. "Maybe when I get some money. I want to get something for my grandpa. He practically raised me since my dad was in and out of jail."

"How about tonight? My treat."

Her eyebrows went up in surprise, then furrowed. "I couldn't. It's too expensive."

I chuckled. "Sweetheart, you won me thirty-five hundred bucks. I'd say I owe you."

She smiled. "Okay. Let's do it."

I grinned back at her. "Okay."

After we ate, we hopped back on the bike, and I took Dixyn to my tattoo guy. The door chimed as we walked in. "Hey, Otto!" I greeted enthusiastically.

The older, tattooed man grinned. "Bullet. Always good to see you." He stood and came over to greet us. "What can I do for you?"

I looked at Dixyn. "Popping this one's cherry and getting a little something for myself."

His eyes lit up as he glanced at Dixyn. "Is that so?" He rubbed his hands together with glee. "Well, I love popping cherries."

Dixyn laughed as Otto asked, "What did you have in mind?"

"I want to get something to honor my grandfather. He passed away recently."

"My condolences. Do you have an idea of what you want to get?"

"Something for our heritage, but not exactly sure what."

We all stood in silence for a second, trying to think of an idea. Then it suddenly hit me: her car, her heritage, her bright red locks. "A firebird."

Dixyn looked at me and smiled. "That's perfect. I love it."

I tucked a strand of her hair behind her ear. "Suits you, my fiery phoenix."

Her cheeks flushed as a grin crept over her lips. Otto tapped the front counter. "I'll get something drawn up for you."

Dixyn and I sat on one of the couches. I draped my arm around her and pulled her against me. "Nervous?"

"A little. You think I can watch you first?"

I smirked at her. "Sure. Whatever you want."

Otto came back with a design, which Dixyn approved, then I described what I wanted, "Mine is simple. I want the number 9 from a roulette wheel with the ball on it." I smiled fondly at Dixyn. "She won me thirty-five hundred on it."

Otto nodded. "Nice. Where you want it?"

I chuckled, eyes still locked with Dixyn's. "I don't know. I'm running out of room."

Dixyn bit down on her lower lip. "Maybe we should see what we're working with."

I arched a brow as I slipped off my cut. "If you wanted to see me naked, sweetheart, all you had to do was ask."

She playfully rolled her eyes as I set my cut on the counter. I pulled off my shirt next, then spread my arms out. I was covered from shoulder to fingers, and my club tattoo took up most of my back. My chest and stomach were pretty much covered, too.

Dixyn pursed her lips as her eyes ran over me, then she met my eyes with a mischievous grin. "Guess you're gonna have to lose the pants, too."

I laughed. "Not until later, kitten." I lifted my arm, gesturing at a free spot on my ribs. "Will this work, Otto?"

He shrugged, eyeing the space. "I can make it work."

I smiled. "My man."

Otto pulled out some paperwork for us to fill out, and I paid for our ink before following him back to his chair. "Who's first?" he asked, slipping on some black gloves.

"Me. She wants to watch first."

Otto readied all his supplies as I laid on my side on the tattoo chair. Dixyn took a seat in front of me and smiled. "Guess you're a pro at this, huh?"

I chuckled. "Yeah. Been getting ink since before you were born."

Her smile fell as her eyes searched mine. "Does my age bother you?"

"Are you serious?" I shook my head with a chuckle. "The fact that a pretty, young thing like you wants me is hot as hell. Any man my age would kill to hook up with you."

She laughed, brightening back up. "Guess you're pretty lucky, old man."

Grabbing her chair, I scooted it closer to me. "I'll show you old man." Then I kissed her, hard and rough. She moaned as I parted her lips with my tongue, kissing her until we were both out of breath. I pulled back to look at her, running my tattooed knuckles down her flushed cheek. Her lips were swollen, and her eyes were heavy with lust.

I smirked. "How's that for an old man?"

She crossed her arms over her chest, trying to suppress a smile. "Okay, I guess."

I loved her sass. She gave as good as she got, and I was going to give it to her good that night. It'd been weeks since I had that pretty pussy, and I planned to make up for lost time.

My tattoo took about three hours. As Otto cleaned and wrapped me up, I asked Dixyn, "Feeling less nervous now?"

Smiling, she nodded. "Yeah, thanks."

Otto took a quick smoke break before setting up for Dixyn's tattoo. "Where you want it, kid?"

"My arm," Dixyn replied, patting her right bicep.

"Good choice." Otto grinned. "Best spot with the least amount of pain."

I took her hand as Otto turned on the tattoo gun. "Squeeze as hard as you need to."

She blew out a shaky breath, then forced a smile. "Okay."

"Ready?" Otto asked as he applied some ointment to Dixyn's arm.

She nodded. "Ready."

As soon as the needle touched her skin, Dixyn flinched, squeezing my hand. She hissed in pain. "Damn, that burns."

Otto and I both chuckled. After a few minutes, Dixyn relaxed. "Okay, that's not so bad."

"The arm is a piece of cake," I said.

She smiled at me. "Thank you for this."

I caressed her hand with my thumb. "Tattoo therapy is the best therapy."

She arched a brow. "You say that like you know from experience."

I tensed. I wasn't going to discuss my demons with her. She couldn't take it. I shrugged, trying to play it off. "Not personally. But some of the guys have mentioned it."

Dixyn's tattoo didn't take as long as mine did, but it still came out badass. Otto had done a traditional Native American-style firebird with black, red, and orange. The colors popped on her skin, and the lines were crisp and clean.

She grinned at her new ink, then up at Otto. "Thank you so much. He would've loved it."

I tipped Otto, then led Dixyn outside. "Ready for a drink?"

"Definitely."

I grabbed her hand and led her to the bar next door to the tattoo shop. I'd been a few times after getting ink, and it was a chill spot. Plus, it wasn't a biker bar, so we didn't have to worry about Kings or Forsaken.

We went inside and took a seat at the bar. There were only a few other people there, so we didn't have to wait to order. "Maker's and a Macallan on the rocks."

Dixyn smiled at me. "I'm surprised you remembered."

"Why?"

She shrugged. "I'm sure you have a ton of club whores. Must be hard to keep track."

I chuckled. "I don't pay attention to them."

The bartender brought our drinks. "You seemed pretty upset when I attacked Barbie."

I scoffed. "I was upset you were causing a scene in front of my brothers. I don't need that drama. That's why I don't have an old lady."

She nodded. "Well, good because I don't want to be one."

I raised my glass to her. "Glad we understand each other."

She tapped my glass with hers, then took a drink. "So where's this going then?"

I arched a brow and smirked. "Hopefully back to my place."

Rolling her eyes, she laughed. Thankfully, she didn't call me out on my response. I didn't want to discuss whatever fucked-up shit we had going on. I just wanted to have some fun with a hot chick and get laid. I told myself that the protectiveness I felt because of the cartel looking for her was because I didn't want someone else touching what was mine, not because I had actual feelings for her.

Because even if she wasn't my old lady, Dixyn was mine.

CHAPTER 11

Dixyn

A fter the bar, Ford took me back to his place. I didn't remember much about it from the first time since I'd been pretty drunk. He had a glorified bachelor pad in a neighborhood on the Colorado River. "Nice view," I commented as I gazed out his sliding glass back door at the water.

"Yeah, it's all right; quiet. You want a drink?"

"Sure." I turned around and arched a brow. "You know what I like."

He smirked as he started fixing us drinks. An amused smiled lifted my lips as I sat on the couch. He probably never had to make drinks since he was the president of one of the most notorious motorcycle clubs in Nevada. I'm sure he had booze handed to him on the regular.

Ford sat next to me and handed me a drink. "It's not Macallan, but it's a decent scotch."

Taking the glass from him, I sipped the iced liquor. "Thank you."

Nodding his head, he took a drink from his glass. He seemed tense. "I don't normally bring chicks back here."

I looked around. There were empty beer bottles, pizza boxes, and dirty laundry scattered everywhere. "I can tell." I laughed.

He chuckled. "Sorry about the mess."

I took another drink and shrugged. "I grew up in a house full of male bikers. I live with three now. I'm used to it. It doesn't bother me."

He looked at me long and hard for a few seconds, then took my glass and set it down on the coffee table with his before kissing me. Every time his lips touched mine, he set me on fire, and I wanted nothing more than to be consumed by the flames.

I climbed onto his lap, never taking my mouth from his. Grinding against him, I pressed my aching sex against his hardened erection. I'd wanted him since I'd gotten on the back of his bike when he'd pick me up, so I was on the brink of exploding with desire.

He slipped his cut off before ripping my shirt down the middle. Our movements were frantic as I pulled off his muscle shirt, tossing it while he gripped my ass and stood, carrying me to his bedroom.

My lips hurt from the rough nips and presses of Ford's mouth and teeth. He tossed me on the bed, then stood over me at the edge. "Lose the rest of the clothes. Now," he gruffly demanded.

Ford unbuckled his jeans as I shimmied out of mine. His cock was at full attention as I crawled over to him. It'd been weeks since we'd hooked up last, and I couldn't wait to have him inside me again.

Looking up at him, I took as much of him in my mouth as I could, suppressing a gag. Ford's eyes rolled back, and he buried his fingers in the hair at the back of my head, urging me to go deeper.

"Fuck," he growled as I increased my pace. I wanted to make him come as quick as possible so that we could move on to round two.

We moved in sync as I sucked Ford off. Only a few minutes passed before he groaned, filling my mouth with his cum.

I pulled back and swallowed, licking my lips. He was on me before I could blink, pushing me down on the bed and filling me with his cock. I gasped as he stretched me, seating himself fully inside me.

"Goddamn, Dixyn," he hissed, his eyes fluttering closed. "Fuck, you fit so perfect around my cock."

A moan escaped me. I hadn't realized how much I'd missed him until that moment. The sensation of his body atop mine, his cock inside me, the fire he lit in my veins. I was about to come undone right then and there.

He slowly pumped in and out of me, taking his time reacquainting our bodies. I wrapped my legs around him, forcing him deeper inside me. "God, I missed this pussy, kitten. I can't get enough of your sweet cunt."

He pounded harder but kept his languid pace. Usually, our sex was rough and fast, but tonight, we weren't in a public place or in a sloppy, drunken rush.

Closing my eyes, I tipped my head back as Ford sucked and nipped at my neck. I raked my nails down his back, and he hissed in pain against my skin before biting my collarbone. I gasped from the painful sensation, my sex clenching even more from the pleasure.

"You gonna come for me, baby?" Ford murmured huskily as he pulled himself out and slammed back into me. "You gonna soak my cock with your sweetness?"

Ford captured my lips as I moaned my response. His dirty talk drove me crazy, and I loved every lust-filled word.

Thrust after blissful thrust, Ford steadily built up my climax until I thought I'd explode. I writhed beneath his beautiful, hardened body, about to burst from the immense pleasure.

"That's it, kitten. Come for me," Ford growled against my lips as he increased his pace, slamming his cock faster and harder into my aching sex.

I dug my nails into his shoulders as he sent me spiraling into oblivion, stars shooting behind my lids as pleasure exploded throughout my limbs. "Oh, God, Ford, yes! Yes, yes, yes!"

A few seconds later, I felt the warmth of his cum streaming onto my stomach. In the heat of the moment, we'd forgotten to use a condom, and I was glad he thought to pull out because I hadn't been able to refill my birth control since leaving LA.

He fell on the bed next to me, panting heavily. His body gleamed with sweat and he looked so goddamn sexy, I was ready for round two.

I wiped his cum off my stomach with his muscle shirt and tossed it to the floor. He watched me as I mounted him, a sexy smirk curving his lips.

I could feel his cock hardening under me as I smiled down at him. "My turn."

After we finished, I laid with my head in the crook of Ford's neck, tracing my fingers along the ink on his chest. "What's this one for?"

He tucked his chin down, trying to see which one I was referring to. "That one's for this run we did through the mountains. We'd been tailing this guy for a few days, and he decided to hide out up there. It was an adventure, to say the least." He chuckled fondly.

I ran my fingers over the mountain tattoo. "My grandpa used to take us up to Spirit Mountain all the time when we were kids. We'd camp overnight, and he told us stories about the constellations and the land. He said it brought us closer to our ancestors. It was my favorite thing to do when I was little."

Ford tucked a piece of hair behind my ear. "You really miss him, huh?"

My chest tightened as a swell of emotion came over me. I sighed, fighting back the pinprick of tears. "Yeah. He was the best part of me."

He rubbed my back affectionately. "I don't know. You have some pretty great parts."

I rolled my eyes and laughed, smacking Ford on the chest. Pulling me closer, he kissed the top of my head. I cuddled up to his side, draping my leg over his stomach. I sighed and closed my eyes, losing myself in the feel of his arms around me. After a few moments of blissful silence, I asked, "What are we doing, Ford?"

His fingers feathered over my back. "I don't know, kitten, but I don't want to stop."

"Me either," I whispered, snuggling my head in the crook of his neck.

Wanting to change the awkward subject, I ran my fingers along a rounded scar that I'd felt when I'd been playing with his arm. He had several spread over his body, but they were camouflaged by his tattoos so they weren't visible unless you were really looking for them. "How'd you get this?"

He glanced away and frowned, avoiding my eyes. "One of my mom's many boyfriends. He liked to burn his cigars out on me."

My heart ached for him. "I'm so sorry."

He didn't say anything, so I blurted out, "My mom was a meth-head prostitute. She overdosed when I was a baby."

Ford looked at me, and a sad smile tipped the corners of his mouth. "Sounds like we both have some pretty fucked-up parents."

I chuckled. "Yeah. It's pretty sad when the better parent is an ex-con biker who owns a strip club and deals guns and drugs."

Ford laughed. I loved the rich, gravelly sound. "Well, at least your dad stuck around. Mine was some rich suit looking for a Vegas fling and wanted nothing to do with my mom or me."

My stomach knotted. Since getting to know little things about Ford, my feelings for him were growing. "What an asshole. I hate pricks like that."

"Yeah. I learned the hard way that family isn't always blood. My brothers are my family; not my mom and not that piece of shit sperm donor. No one was really there for me before the club. I made myself the man I am today."

I snuggled closer to him, wanting to give him comfort with my touch since I didn't know what to say. I felt him kiss the top of my head. Closing my eyes, I reveled in the feel of his arms around me. I hadn't felt safe since before Matteo, but in Ford's embrace, I knew he'd protect me.

And in the haven of Ford's arms, I easily fell asleep that night.

When I woke up the next morning, I was still in Ford's arms, but he was spooning me instead of cradling me against his side.

And his huge cock was pressing against my ass.

I pushed back against him, a sleepy smile drifting over my lips, and he hummed in appreciation.

His hand snaked down to my center, and as soon as his skilled fingers touched my folds, I got wet.

Ford nibbled my earlobe and pressed his erection against me. "That pussy loves daddy, doesn't she, kitten?"

I tipped my head back and moaned as he sank two fingers inside me. "Yes."

Nipping at my neck, Ford growled against my skin. "I'm gonna finger-fuck this pussy until you beg me to stop. Then I'm gonna fuck you so hard you won't be able to see straight."

That sounded like the perfect way to start the day in my opinion.

After Ford kept his promise, we went another round in the shower, then he helped me properly clean my tattoo and put ointment on it.

"How does it feel?" he asked as I got dressed.

"Like a sunburn." My arm was tight and stung where my new tattoo was.

He chuckled. "That's a good way to describe it."

I smiled at him. He was so handsome, especially when he let his guard down.

"I've gotta go to the shop. Need a ride back to your car?"

I looked at him in the mirror as I braided my hair to the side. "That would be nice."

Ford smiled fondly at me. He was already dressed in a white tee shirt, black jeans, and his cut. "There's coffee if you need it. It's about all I have here for breakfast."

I giggled. "Yeah, I'll grab a cup."

After I got dressed and freshened up, we drank a cup of coffee together before we left. When Ford pulled up next to my car in the casino parking lot, I hopped off, slipping off the helmet and handing it to him. "Thanks."

He smacked me on the ass and grinned. "See you later?"

I smiled. "If you're lucky, old man."

He chuckled before revving the bike and driving away. I unlocked my car and got in, sighing. Ford made me happy, and that scared the shit out of me. I didn't need to go falling for him, but I didn't see how not to unless we stopped seeing each other, and I didn't want that.

We were both being selfish and reckless. He was going against club politics, and I was going against my family. But neither one of us seemed to care. Not only was the sex mind-blowing, but I had a good time with him. He wasn't afraid to call me on my shit and put me in my place when I needed it, and that was hot as hell. He treated my body like a temple and knew exactly how to worship me like I deserved. No other man had even come close to making me feel the way he did.

Like an addict, I knew what I was doing wasn't good for me, but I couldn't stop. I'd had a hit and wanted as much as I could get, no matter if the result would be ugly. And there was no way it couldn't be. Blood would most likely be spilled, and that would be on my hands unless I was smart about what we were doing.

Everything had to be secret: meetings, conversations, stolen moments. Neither of us could tell anyone, not even those we trusted most; it would be too risky. And I didn't want anyone getting hurt because of our selfishness.

I drove home, feeling confident with my decision. I was sure Ford would agree that if we were going to continue doing what we were doing, we needed discretion and secrecy in order for anything to work. I just hoped it didn't bite us in the ass in the end.

I was surprised to find my dad home when I pulled up. He typically spent most of his time at the strip club or clubhouse, and I rarely saw him now that I was working. "Hey, Dad."

At first, my dad smiled at me, but his eyes narrowed as they fell on my tattoo. "What the hell is that on your arm?"

"I got a tattoo for Grandpa," I replied.

His expression softened as he walked over to me. "Let me take a look."

I held out my arm for him to see. He carefully gripped it as he inspected my new ink.

"Do you think Grandpa would've liked it?" I asked, hoping for validation of my choice.

He grinned. "He would've loved it, sweetheart. It's perfect."

Pride swelled within me, knowing my grandpa would've approved of my tribute to him. I had to take a deep breath to fight the tears pricking my eyes.

My dad let go of my arm. "Who'd you go with?"

Shit. I hadn't prepared for an interrogation. I quickly thought up a lie, my acting skills coming in handy. "Nina. We went after work, then I crashed back at her place."

He nodded, seeming to accept my answer. "Want some coffee?"

"Sure," I responded. I needed another cup after the night I'd had with Ford. We only got a few hours of sleep, and I had a busy day ahead of me.

I sat down at the table. "Where are Raleigh and Jameson?"

My dad answered me from the kitchen, "Out on a run. They should be back in a couple of days."

"Oh." I didn't really care to know details about what my brothers did in the club because it only made me worry more about them.

A few moments later, my dad sat next to me and handed me a mug. "Thanks," I said before blowing on the steaming liquid.

"There's something I want to talk to you about."

Shit.

My stomach dropped as I set my coffee down, trying to play it cool. "Okay, what is it?"

"Remember that morning you came home hungover? You flinched when I went to grab you."

That was the morning after the first time Ford and I hooked up. "Yeah. What about it?"

"We haven't really had the chance to talk since you started working, but I told you that conversation wasn't over."

I took a sip of my coffee, waiting for him to continue. His face hardened in anger as he leaned forward on the table. "Has someone been hurting you, Dixyn?"

I sighed, then crossed my arms over my chest. "Not anymore."

His fists clenched as he growled, "Who?"

"This guy back in LA."

He placed a hand on my shoulder. "Why didn't you tell me? I could've helped you."

I shook my head, fighting back tears. "He's dangerous."

He slammed a fist down on the table, making me jump. "I'm dangerous!" he yelled before lowering his voice to a harsh whisper. "No one touches my daughter. I will tear that motherfucker apart for hurting my baby girl. Now, tell me who he is."

I shook my head again, afraid for my family. I knew my dad would get the club involved, and I didn't want that blood on my hands.

My dad firmly gripped me by the shoulders. "Dixie, the club and I can take care of this asshole for you. He'll never hurt you again."

The tears started falling. "You don't understand. He's not just some normal guy."

There was fire in his eyes as they locked onto mine. "I don't care if he's the goddamn president. I will slit his fucking throat."

I took a deep breath to compose myself and shook my head. "I can't. I can't risk you or Raleigh or Jameson. I can't lose you."

My dad cupped my cheek, his face softening. "Who'd you get involved with, Dixie girl?"

"It doesn't matter. I got away." I took his large hands in mine and squeezed. "You'll protect me, right?"

"Of course, sweetheart. Always."

I threw my arms around my dad's neck and hugged him tightly. We didn't have the best history, but I knew deep down that my dad would take care of me.

He wrapped me in his embrace, and cursed, "Dammit, Dixyn."

I let him hold me for a few minutes before I pulled away. "Thank you, Daddy."

He grinned. "I will find out who this motherfucker is. Then I'm going to kill him."

I didn't respond as I took a sip of my coffee. My dad got up and went into the garage, leaving me with my thoughts. Matteo was good at covering his tracks and used multiple aliases, so I didn't think my dad would be able to link him to me. We didn't have any joint bills or accounts, he always gave me cash, and I was never involved in important business. There was nothing to tie us together.

My dad was stubborn, though. He was probably making calls trying to dig up information at that very moment.

I finished my coffee and sighed. My thoughts turned to Ford, and I wondered what he would do if he found out about Matteo. Would he be as pissed as my dad? Did he care about me enough to seek retribution?

I pushed the thoughts aside. I didn't want to even entertain the idea that Matteo would ever be back in my life in any way, and that included the people I cared about trying to find him. The last thing I needed was anyone getting hurt or killed because of me.

Later that day, Nina, Hannah, and I were at a bridal shop looking at dresses for the wedding.

"What do you think of this one?" Hannah asked.

I scrunched my face. "Too many ruffles."

"Hey, I like ruffles," Hannah defended, placing both hands on her hips defensively.

"I agree with Dee. I like ruffles, too, but there is such a thing as too much."

Hannah deflated, huffing. "Fine. I'll try on the next one."

As she went back into the dressing room, Nina asked, "So how's your forbidden biker?"

I shrugged, trying to play it off. "I don't know. Haven't seen him."

Nina pinched me. "You dirty, dirty liar. I know he came to the casino looking for you yesterday."

I rubbed my arm where she pinched me and frowned. "Okay, okay. We hooked up, but that was the last time."

Nina smiled triumphantly. "Mm-hmm. Just like the time at the poker game was the last time. Keep telling yourself that."

"I'm serious," I hissed. "There's no way it can work without someone getting hurt, and I can't have that on my hands."

"I'm sure that cock is nice in your hands, though." She arched a brow and gave me a mischievous grin. "I caught a glimpse of it at the strip club that night, and let me just say, damn."

I smacked her arm, then pointed a finger at her. "No. That's my dick. Don't even think about it."

She raised her hands in surrender. "I know. I wouldn't do something like that to you. I'm just saying I don't know how you could give that up."

Tell me about it.

"It's just dick," I lied. "There are plenty out there. Plus, I need to focus on work and preparing for school."

Nina nodded. "Good. Glad that's settled then."

Hannah came out in the next gown, and my jaw dropped.

"Holy shit," Nina blurted out.

Hannah had a huge smile on her face as she twirled around in the beautiful ball gown. It was off-white with a sweetheart neckline embroidered with intricate lace and rhinestones that covered the whole bodice. The bottom was like something out of a fairy tale with more lace and rhinestones.

"That's it," I stated.

"You think?" Hannah asked, staring at herself in one of the full-length mirrors.

I nodded. "Definitely."

"Hell yeah," Nina agreed. "You look beautiful, Hannah."

"Absolutely gorgeous. Meghan is going to be blown away."

Hannah squealed, eyes glossy with happiness. "Yay. Let me get out of this, and we'll go grab lunch."

After Hannah finalized her dress with her wedding planner, we went to a nearby bistro to eat lunch.

"I'm so glad I have you guys to help me with all this wedding planning. I don't know what I'd do without you."

I smiled. I'd missed the camaraderie of girlfriends. "Of course. I know I wouldn't miss it."

Nina mumbled around a bite of her food. "Yeah, what she said."

We all laughed. "You're going with Meghan to pick out hers, too, right?"

"Yeah. Next weekend, I think." I looked at Nina for confirmation, but she shrugged. I shook my head with a laugh. She was more disorganized than I was.

"Good. Her other friends haven't been the most understanding. Most thought it was just a phase." She shrugged, a deflated frown on her face.

"Well, fuck them. If they don't accept your relationship, they're not real friends," Nina said.

I reached across the table and placed my hand on her arm. "We're here for both of you. Always."

She smiled as she glanced back and forth between Nina and me. "I love you guys."

Before finishing up lunch, we made plans to meet with a caterer after Meghan's dress fitting the following weekend.

As Nina and I walked to our cars, she asked, "You want to come over tonight? Watch some Netflix, order pizza, drink some wine?"

I smiled. Having a relaxing girls' night was just what I needed. "Sure. Count me in."

CHAPTER 12

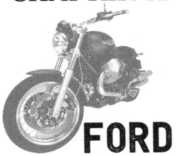

FORD

The next day at church, we discussed the lingering presence of the cartel in Laughlin. They hadn't made any moves against us, but two things bothered me from them being there; one, my prospect still hadn't been able to confirm if Dixyn was the redhead they were looking for, and two, I didn't want them trying to deal in my territory.

"We need to find out what they're doing here and get them the hell out of Laughlin. This is our town. We don't need cartel scum hanging around," I said, annoyed we hadn't found out more information. "I want intel by tomorrow, and I want them out of here by next week. Am I clear?" I asked, locking eyes with each of my men around the table.

They all nodded.

"Good; glad that's settled. Now, we got a bounty job." I opened the file folder given to me by the client and set it in the middle of the table. "Client wants this to be clean and quiet. The mark was last seen around Lake Mead. Will probably take a couple of days, maybe a week. The mark is an investment banker who stiffed the wrong bookie for over fifty grand." I glanced up and stated, "Kojack and Hook, take Deuce and find this guy. Keep it clean and make sure no one finds the body."

The three men nodded as Kojack replied, "Got it."

I slid the file to Kojack, then went on to the next agenda item. "We got a decent order from the Kingsmen up in Vegas; about a dozen AR's and Glocks. AK, how's our stock looking?"

"We have enough to fill the order, but we'll need to restock after. I'll contact the Chinks for another shipment."

We got our guns from the Chinese via the Long Beach port. "Good. Keep me updated. Anything else?" When no one else brought up any other business, I banged the gavel to end the meeting.

As the men filed out, I asked for Trey and Dead Man to hang back. Once everyone else had left and the door was closed, I asked, "What's the latest?"

Trey shook his head. "Nothin' new. They've mostly been speaking in Spanish to the Mexican locals, so I can't make out what they're talking about."

"Dammit," I cursed. My mind raced as I thought about our next move. "We're gonna have to grab one of them."

Dead Man nodded. "I'll set it up. We've only seen three or four around, but they usually travel in pairs. Should be an easy snatch."

"Keep it quiet," I instructed. "Tonight. I want one of those wetbacks here by sunrise."

"Got it, boss," Dead Man said as he draped an arm around Trey's shoulders. "Let's go, kid."

After they left, I lit a cigarette to ease my nerves. I was anxious because we hadn't found out more about the cartel's motives, and I wanted to get them the hell out of my city. I didn't like being in the dark; I typically knew everything happening in and around Laughlin, and I preferred to keep it that way.

I decided to head to Harlot's to have a few drinks and get my mind off our cartel issue. When I entered, I went straight to the bar where Dimes, Cowboy, and Ajax were already sitting. I nodded my head at them. "Hey."

The bartender set down a cold tall boy in front of me, and I grinned. "You read my mind." I took a long swig and set the glass down. "Ah."

The guys and I started shooting the shit as Tammy came up to me, draping an arm around my shoulder. "Hey, Bullet."

I barely gave her a second glance. She was hot, but all I could think about was Dixyn and her tight cunt and fat ass. "Hey, sweetheart."

I went back to talking to the guys, but Tammy didn't take the hint. "I was thinking we could talk," she said suggestively, running her perfectly manicured finger down the front of my cut.

I took another drink, then chuckled. "If you want to talk, then talk."

My brothers laughed, and Tammy forced a smile. "In private."

I knew what private things she wanted to "talk" about, but for the first time, I wasn't interested. Dixyn had kept me up all night and fully sated me, which was saying something. She'd milked every last drop and then some. I made eye contact, making sure Tammy knew I meant business. "I'm busy. Maybe later."

I downed the rest of my beer as she spat, "You know, ever since that redhead slut came around, you've been a real asshole."

All laughter and conversation stopped. My blood was boiling as I whipped my hand out and grabbed Tammy by the throat. "You watch your tongue, cunt."

I could feel all eyes on us, but I knew no one would interfere. Everyone else knew their place, but obviously Tammy needed reminding. Her eyes were wide with fear as she gripped my forearm tightly. "No one asked for your opinion. The only thing you need to open your mouth for is to put my dick in it, and that's if I let you. Understand?"

She answered with a frantic nod.

"Good. Now get the fuck out of my sight." I let her go, and she stumbled back before scurrying to the exit and out the door.

The guys laughed and conversation around the bar resumed as normal. I signaled the bartender for another beer, and she quickly poured it for me.

"Thanks, doll."

Ajax and I were playing our third round of pool when my phone buzzed. The text was from Dead Man.

Dead Man: *Got the package. Headed to the warehouse.*

I smiled. Finally, some good news. I messaged him back.

Me: *Good. Omw*

I put my pool cue back on the rack. "Got some business to deal with. Catch y'all later, boys."

I headed to the warehouse where we'd made the exchange with the cartel. Occasionally, we also used it for more unsavory business dealings like when we needed to interrogate someone or get rid of a body.

When I pulled up, I saw the shop van already there, and my body buzzed with nervous energy. I wanted answers and wasn't afraid to do what was needed to get them.

I went inside and locked the door behind me. Dead Man and Trey were in the center of the warehouse, tying a man to a chair. His mouth had duct tape over it, and he had a cut above his eye that was bleeding down the side of his face.

Dead Man looked up when I walked over. "Any problems?" I asked.

He shook his head. "Nah. This guy went to the corner store near their hotel alone. Was easy to grab him and take him out the back."

"Good. No one tailed you?"

"No. We took a lot of backroads to make sure."

Trey stepped back after he finished tying the guy's legs. He was yelling, but I couldn't make out what he was saying because his words were muffled from the duct tape.

I gestured around the room. "These walls are soundproof. No one is going to hear you here."

Being in the types of businesses we dealt in, we had to take precautions to make sure we didn't draw unwanted attention. That was why we had the warehouse out in the middle of nowhere and even went to the trouble of soundproofing the walls, as well, just to be safe.

His eyes narrowed, and he continued to try to yell through the duct tape.

"Suit yourself." I sighed, then laughed. "I'm going to ask you a few questions. Your answers will determine how long you're stuck here and how badly I hurt you."

I began to pace back and forth in front of him. "What's the name of the girl you're looking for?"

I gestured to Trey to remove the duct tape. When he did, the man started screaming for help and cursing in Spanish.

I blew out a breath of exasperation, letting him scream a few minutes before punching him in the jaw. That shut him up.

"I'm gonna ask you again. Who is the girl you're looking for?"

He spit blood on the concrete floor. "Fuck you, *puto*."

I chuckled. I hadn't given a good beating in a while. "Wrong answer."

I punched him in the left eye, giving him a matching gash to the opposite eye. "We're not letting you go until you tell me what I want to know." I grabbed a rusted metal bucket that was underneath a nearby table and held it up for him to see. "You see this right here? This is your bathroom for the time that you're here."

His eyes widened a little, which made me smirk. "The sooner you talk, the sooner you can be on your way. Now, who is the girl you're looking for?"

He didn't respond for several seconds, and I thought he was going to crack. Then he chuckled. "*Chupa mi verga.*"

Since we dealt with the cartel for years, I'd learned some Spanish along the way, primarily the cuss words. So him telling me to suck his dick pissed me the fuck off. I punched him so hard that I made the chair fall over from the momentum.

He grunted as he hit the concrete, and I kicked him in the stomach for good measure, making him groan in pain.

I lit a cigarette and took a drag to ease my nerves. I was close to completely losing my cool, but I needed to keep my composure before I ended up beating the guy to death. It wouldn't be the first time, but I preferred to keep the cops off my back.

I blew out smoke as Trey righted the chair. I took another drag as I stared at the guy, calculating the best way to get through to him.

"I don't know if you've ever been in this situation before, but I have. You may think that if you don't talk we'll eventually let you go. Or maybe you're stupid enough to think that one of your spick friends will come find you." I took a few steps toward him and leaned down until we were eye to eye. "No one will find you out here. The only way you're getting out of here is if I let you go. And you don't want to know what the alternative is." I let my eyes drift to some of the barrels of acid we had against the wall.

His gaze followed mine, and when they settled on the barrels, there was no denying his fear. He brought his eyes back to mine, staring me down for a few seconds. Then he spat in my face.

After the few seconds of shock, I was filled with rage. No one spat in my face and got away with it. I let out a roar of anger and burned my cigarette out in his eye.

He screamed in pain as I held it there. "I'm not playing games with you. Either you start talking or I start chopping fingers off."

I tossed the cigarette, then went to the bathroom to wash my face and calm down. When I came back, the guy's eye was swollen shut and red. "That looks pretty bad." I chuckled, lighting another cigarette and taking a drag. "Want me to do the other?"

He frantically shook his head. "No. Please, no." Finally, I was getting somewhere.

"Then tell me what I want to know."

He shook his head, whining like a pussy. "I can't. He'll kill me."

I scoffed. "I'll kill you. But I'll do it slower and more painfully."

Crying, he shook his head again. I felt a little bad for the guy, but then I thought about Dixyn and him spitting in my face. "I'm going to give you until tomorrow to tell me. If you don't, then the real fun will start."

I turned my attention to Trey. "Stay here. Don't let him out of your sight."

"Got it, Pres."

Dead Man and I went outside. "He'll break by tomorrow," Dead Man said.

I nodded. "The sooner the better."

The fear I had for Dixyn's safety was a foreign emotion for me. The only people I cared about were my brothers, so for me to be feeling the way I was said something about how I felt about her, no matter how much I denied it.

Dead Man got in the van. "I'm heading to Harlot's. See you there?"

I finished off my cigarette and dropped it to the ground before snuffing it out with my boot. "Yeah, maybe."

He gave me a knowing smile. "Okay, brother."

He drove off, leaving me with my thoughts. I wanted to see Dixyn, but I didn't want things between us getting more serious than they were. Distance was key in keeping our arrangement simple. Great sex and a good time; nothing more.

Then why did I have a cartel roach tied up in my warehouse trying to get answers about her?

I pushed the thoughts to the back of my mind. Any information about what the cartel was doing was vital to staying on top, especially since our business deal had gone south. We needed to know as much as we could about what they were doing and who they had interest in. And if that included Dixyn, we needed to know about it.

I told myself it was just business, but deep down, I knew that was bullshit.

CHAPTER 13

Dixyn

The weekend after Hannah's dress fitting, the girls and I were at a local catering company taste-testing different menu options for the wedding.

As the caterer went back to get the next round of samples, I asked Hannah, "So what do you think?"

She pursed her lips. "It's good, but I haven't been wowed by anything yet. Am I being too picky?"

"No." I scoffed. "This is your wedding we're talking about here."

Meghan placed her hand on top of Hannah's. "You deserve whatever you want. And this isn't our only option. We also have that all-inclusive place to visit next weekend."

Hannah sighed, smiling at her fiancée. "You're right. There are always other options."

"And wasn't D'Angelo's also on the table?" I asked, remembering what they had said at dinner when I'd first gotten back.

"Yes. We still have to set up a tasting with them, too," Meghan stated. "Don't worry, babe."

My phone chimed with a text. Nina, Meghan, and Hannah were chatting about more wedding stuff as I glanced at the message, and a smile curved my lips.

Ford: *You free tonight kitten?*

Me: *I have to work until ten, but I'm free after that*

Ford: *Perfect. I'll pick you up. Pack a bag.*

My brows furrowed. What was he up to?

Me: *Ok*

Nina leaned over, and whispered, "I know that look. Someone's talking to a certain forbidden biker."

I scoffed, putting my phone away. "No, I'm not."

"Someone's getting dicked down tonight," Nina joked with a laugh.

I felt my cheeks heat, shaking my head. "You're ridiculous."

"It's not ridiculous if it's true," Meghan pointed out.

I let out a huff but didn't respond to their comments about Ford. "So what's the final verdict?"

Thankfully, Hannah went along with my change of subject. "I want to try some other options before deciding anything."

"Good idea," I agreed.

We finished up with the caterer, then I went home to change for work and pack a bag for whatever Ford had planned for that night. Excitement hummed through me as I thought about what Ford had up his sleeve.

"You going somewhere?" Raleigh asked.

I glanced up to see him leaning against my doorframe. "Just going to Nina's after work."

An amused smile lifted his lips. "You stay over there a lot. You two still hook up?"

I threw a pillow at him. "That's none of your business."

He chuckled as he swatted the pillow away. "That's a yes."

I scoffed, then thought of something to piss him off and shut him up. "Oh yeah. A few weeks after I got back, we hooked up with this cowboy, and he was fucking Nina from behind as she—"

Raleigh held up his hand, closing his eyes. "Stop. Okay, okay, I get it. I won't ask any more questions."

I grinned, pleased with his embarrassment. "Good. I wouldn't want to tell you about the time with the dildo and two frat boys."

He put his hands over his ears, then turned and walked away. "La, la, la, la, la!" he yelled, drowning me out.

I fell on the bed in a fit of giggles. Torturing older brothers was fun.

I waited for Ford outside after my shift. He pulled up a few minutes after ten and stopped the bike in front of me and got off. Butterflies swarmed my stomach as he slipped off his helmet and ran a hand through his hair to get it out of his face. "Hey," he greeted.

My cheeks heated as a cheesy grin spread over my face. Ford had me feeling like I was back in high school with some silly crush. "Hey."

He took my bag and secured it on the back of his bike, then handed me a helmet. "Hop on."

I slipped the helmet on and got on behind him. Once I wrapped my arms around him, we drove off.

"Where are we going?" I yelled.

"A surprise," he yelled back.

I shook my head. I should've known he wasn't going to tell me, but it didn't take long for me to figure out where we were going once we were out of the city.

I clutched him tighter as I gazed at Spirit Mountain getting closer. My chest tightened with emotion as I wondered why he was taking me somewhere so special to me.

We drove up to Grapevine Canyon, where he finally stopped and parked the bike near the small spring that flowed up there. "What are we doing here, Ford?"

He hopped off the bike and took off his helmet. "Camping." He went to the back of the bike and grabbed my bag and one I assumed was his. "I brought snacks, a couple of blankets, beer. Everything we need."

My heart swelled, and I couldn't help but smile. Not falling for Ford was going to be harder than I expected, especially if he continued doing thoughtful shit.

We set up camp, complete with a fire. We sat down on one of the blankets Ford had laid out, and he dug through his bag, pulled out a beer, and handed it to me.

"This is not what I expected when you told me to pack a bag."

He chuckled as he grabbed a beer for himself. "Well, I hope it was a good surprise."

I stared at him, the light from the flames dancing over his handsome, rugged face. "Yeah, it was. Thank you."

He smiled and tucked a strand of hair behind my ear. "You're welcome."

After a couple of beers, Ford laid down and stared up at the stars. "Tell me one of your grandpa's stories."

I finished my beer and laid down next to him with a sigh. My eyes scanned the night sky as I searched for the Big Dipper. "My favorite is about the Big Dipper," I said, pointing at the constellation. "My grandpa said that according to legend, a great bear was pursued by three Indian braves. The chase began at the beginning of time when the first Indian shot and struck the bear in the side with his bow and arrow. The wound wasn't fatal, so the bear kept running. He has been running across the sky ever since."

I could see Ford watching me out of the corner of my eye, so I continued, "The bear's path changes from season to season. In the fall, he begins low in the northwest. During this season, the arrow wound of the bear opens slightly, and a little blood trickles down upon the land. It covers the leaves of the trees and dyes them red, and that is why we have autumn."

"That's morbid," Ford commented. "You learned this when you were a kid?"

I chuckled. "It does seem kinda morbid now that I look back on it, but when we were little, my brothers and I would pretend to be the three Indian braves and my grandpa would be the bear." I laughed as I remembered the times we'd act out the story. "He was so great at it. He'd roar and grunt just like a bear and was so dramatic whenever he got shot. My sides would hurt from laughing so much." I let out a whimsical sigh. "I'll never forget that."

We stared up at the twinkling stars, bright and vibrant without any light pollution. "I really love it out here." I turned my head to look at him, and he did the same, smiling warmly at me. "Thank you for bringing me."

We stared in each other's eyes a few seconds before Ford bridged the distance between us, crushing my lips with his.

He parted my lips with his tongue and climbed on top of me, pressing his erection against my sex.

I moaned in his mouth from the pressure pushing against my clit. We stripped our clothes until we were skin to skin with nothing between us.

"God, you're so fucking beautiful," Ford murmured against my lips before nipping them. His cock pressed against my soaked pussy, dripping with want for him. "You're mine. You hear me, kitten? Mine."

And then he slammed himself inside me, making us both groan with pleasure. "Yes," I whimpered in agreement. "I'm yours."

Ford slowly pounded in and out of me. "That's right, baby. This pussy is mine. All fucking mine."

I had no idea if he was just caught up in the moment or serious, but I didn't care. All I wanted was Ford for as long as I could have him.

Ford tore his mouth from mine and moved to my neck, kissing and nipping the sensitive skin. "First, I'm gonna claim this pussy." He nibbled on my earlobe, then growled, "Then I'm claiming that ass."

His words fueled my desire, bringing me closer to climax. I moaned his name, unable to think of anything other than him.

I felt his fingers playing with my asshole, and I tensed.

"You ever let anyone in this ass before, kitten?"

"No," I answered breathlessly, caught up in lust.

He let out the sexiest chuckle. "Good."

He continued to thrust into me as he slipped a finger in my forbidden entrance. I'd done some ass play before, but never full penetration, and I was both excited and scared.

As soon as his finger and cock moved together in sync, my body exploded in the most intense orgasm I'd ever had. "Oh, God, Ford!"

Ford captured the rest of my moan with his mouth as I came undone, shuddering with bliss.

"Fuck, you're gushing. So fucking wet," he growled as he pumped in and out of me. A few seconds later, he came with a roar that echoed in the silent night, claiming me just like he'd said.

He collapsed next to me as our heavy breaths filled the calm of the desert night. "Fuck, kitten," he panted between breaths.

I was still dazed with lust as Ford turned me on my side and propped one of my legs up. I felt his fingers at my entrance, playing with our combined wetness.

I glanced at him. He was on his knees behind me, gazing down at me with lidded eyes and a sexy smirk. With just the stars and the moonlight behind him, he looked like an ethereal fallen angel.

He moistened my asshole with our cum. "I'll be gentle at first, sweetheart, but I'm claiming every part of you tonight." His eyes were heavy with desire. "Nothing will be gentle about it when I'm finished. There won't be any doubt that you're mine."

Damn, I was so turned on even though I knew it was going to hurt. There was something about anal that was so primal and raw, and I wanted my first experience to be with Ford. We had a connection that I didn't understand, but it was unlike anything I'd ever felt before. And he'd probably never admit it, but I knew he felt it too.

He played with me for a few minutes, making sure I was relaxed and lubricated enough before he pressed the head of his cock against my ass. "Eyes on me, kitten," Ford directed.

I brought my gaze to his as he slowly pushed inside me. The pain was intense, and I felt like he was going to rip me open, which made me start to panic.

He linked our fingers together. "Keep your eyes on me, baby. Stay with me."

I focused on his beautiful, dark eyes again and felt myself relax. "That's my girl. Just stay focused on me."

He slowly pumped in and out of my ass. Once I relaxed and adjusted to him being inside me in that foreign way, pleasure hummed through me. I felt exposed and erotic, letting him have me like that, and I'd never been more turned on.

Ford increased his pace, and I couldn't stop the moans that escaped me. Our eyes were locked as he pounded into me, and I'd never felt more connected to someone.

His free hand found my clit, and he started to play with the sensitive bud. "I love how wet you get for me, kitten."

Another orgasm hit me hard and fast, and I cried out Ford's name as he continued to claim me. He gripped my hips, thrusting harder as he growled. "You're mine. This pussy, this ass; all mine."

My limbs were tingling with ecstasy as my eyes fluttered shut.

The pain Ford was subjecting me to was something I never thought I'd enjoy. I didn't know how something could hurt so much and feel so good at the same time. The way he was claiming me was so goddamn sexy, and I loved how alpha he was.

He came with a guttural groan, stilling behind me as his fingers dug into my hips. After a few seconds, he pulled out of me, making me gasp from the strange sensation of the sudden loss of fullness.

Ford wrapped his arms around me and pulled me against him. Naked bodies pressed together, he kissed my temple and covered us with another blanket before nuzzling his face into my hair. "You're gonna be the death of me, Dixyn."

The blissful smile I had fell. I was afraid he was right.

Ford took me back to his place to get cleaned up when we woke up. We'd fallen asleep naked in each other's arms with just the blanket and moonlight covering us. It was the most romantic night I'd ever experienced, which was ironic since Ford was a hard-ass biker, and he'd fucked me in the ass.

He took me back to my car after I showered and changed. When I handed him my helmet, he grabbed me and pulled me to him before kissing me long and hard. "See you later?"

Wobbling a little from the daze of his kiss, I gripped his long beard and kissed him again, smiling. "If you're lucky."

He grinned at me, making my heart melt as he revved his bike and took off.

I got in my car, wincing as I sat down. A small chuckle escaped me knowing Ford would love the fact that he was affecting me even when we weren't together.

I went home to find both of my brothers and my dad home. Bags filled with guns sat on the table and my stomach filled with dread as they scurried around the house. "What's up?"

Jameson set another duffel on the table. "Have a run; leaving tonight."

My brows pulled together. "All of you? Dad too?"

"Yep," my dad answered. "Big job."

A lump suddenly formed in my throat as unease filled me. "How long will you be gone?"

"A few days; week tops," Raleigh answered. "Not to worry, little sister."

I scoffed. "Easier said than done."

My dad came over and kissed the top of my head. "You won't even know we're gone. You work so much and are over at Nina's most of the time, so you'll be fine."

I felt a pang of guilt for lying about my whereabouts. "It's not me I'm worried about."

My dad chuckled. "We'll be fine. Done this hundreds of times, Dixie girl."

I crossed my arms as I watched them zip up some of the bags. I needed something to keep me busy and keep my mind off them leaving. "At least let me make you a homecooked meal before you go."

My dad grinned at me. "That sounds great, sweetheart. We're not leaving until late, so we've got time for supper."

A little bit of relief washed over me, and I nodded. "Okay, I'll go to the store to grab some stuff."

One of my favorite hobbies was cooking. Back in high school, I'd done most of the cooking at home, especially after my grandma passed away. But once I'd moved away, I didn't get to that much since I'd lived alone.

As I shopped for the ingredients for my favorite lasagna recipe, my thoughts turned to Ford. The night we'd had lingered in the back of my mind and made me want more of my forbidden biker.

He said he'd claimed me, so how deep did that claim go? What did that mean for us?

I'd said I'd never wanted to be an old lady, but that didn't mean that I wanted Ford hooking up with anyone else either. And I'm pretty sure he didn't want me fucking other guys. I needed clarification on what was going on between us to see if he felt the same.

I decided to text him.

Me: *Can you meet me tonight?*

He didn't reply right away. I finished my grocery shopping and was loading the groceries in my car when he texted me back.

Ford: *Sure, kitten. Where and when?*

Me: *Your place?*

Ford: *Ok, I'll meet you there at 11*

Me: *K :)*

Sighing, I finished loading my groceries and drove home. With my dad and brothers going on a run, I didn't have to worry about being caught with Ford as much, but the concern was always there in the back of my mind.

My brothers helped unload the groceries, then I went to work preparing my lasagna. They continued packing their gear and getting things ready for their run as I cooked, and I kinda enjoyed the strange homeyness of it all. Our home life was definitely not your typical picture of normal, but it worked for us.

And that made me wonder if it could work for Ford and me, which was a dangerous train of thought concerning something that was supposed to be casual. Hopefully talking to Ford would give me some clarity on everything because I was confused when it came to what was going on between us. Except when we were together; everything felt perfect in those moments.

After putting the lasagna in the oven, I chopped some greens and tomatoes for a salad and made some garlic bread. Then I set the table and made some fresh lemonade.

My dad walked in as I was taking the lasagna out. "Damn, Dixie, that smells delicious."

I smiled. "Almost ready. Just have to let it cool off."

When the lasagna had cooled and everyone was at the table, we passed around the salad, bread, and pasta, then dug in.

After his first few bites, Jameson commented, "This is fucking great, Dixyn."

Raleigh agreed. "We haven't had food this good since Grandma died."

I smiled proudly as my dad nodded. "It's good to have you back," he said fondly.

My dad and I didn't have the best relationship, and the emotions between us were typically messy. We were both hardheaded and hot-tempered, but we were still family. Even though I still resented him for several things, losing my grandfather made me realize how important family was. "Thanks, Dad."

After the guys had seconds, my brothers helped me clear the table and wash the dishes as my dad loaded their gear. Then we went outside so I could send them off. I gave them each a hug before they mounted their bikes.

"Please be careful," I warned.

"Always," Jameson said with a wink before slipping on his helmet.

"We'll be back soon," my dad assured.

"Don't have too much fun while we're gone," Raleigh joked.

I waved as they drove away, concern making my chest tight and my stomach knot. When I couldn't see their taillights anymore, I went back inside, telling myself they would be okay.

After I put the leftovers away, I went up to my room to get ready to see Ford. The guilt about seeing him was starting to fade, and I wasn't sure if that was a good or a bad thing. I figured only time would tell.

CHAPTER 14

FORD

fter the night I'd had with Dixyn, I felt on top of the world. Claiming her raw like I had out in the desert was one for the books. There was a connection between us I couldn't explain, and I wanted as much as I could get of her, no matter the consequences. And that was bad. Very, very bad.

The cartel asshole we had tied up in the warehouse still hadn't broken yet, and my patience was wearing thin. I'd already cut off three fingers, and he still wasn't talking.

I went to the warehouse after dropping Dixyn off, determined to make the motherfucker talk. After claiming her like I had, I owed it to her to protect her. I wasn't planning on leaving until I got answers.

Trey was reading a motorcycle magazine with his feet propped up on a metal table. He stood as I approached. "He say anything?"

My prospect shook his head. "Stubborn wetback."

My lips curled in anger as I walked over to the cartel prick. It'd been six days, and while I enjoyed torturing the fuck, I preferred getting answers.

He had his head hung, no doubt exhausted and drained. I grabbed the hand I'd cut the fingers off of, and he groaned in pain.

He cursed at me in Spanish as I observed, "This looks pretty bad. Probably infected. You should see a doctor."

"Then let me go," he gritted out. He looked like hell—greasy hair, bags under his eyes, skin caked with dried blood and dirt. We'd only been giving him water and bread every other day to help wear him down and hadn't let him shower.

I squeezed his hand tightly before dropping it. "I don't know how many times I have to tell you this, but you're not leaving until you talk. This is all a result of your choice, and you have the power to make it stop."

He didn't respond. I started to pace back and forth in front of him as I stated, "I think I'm gonna start on the other hand today. Balance you out a little bit."

I pulled my knife from my side and held it out. His eyes widened as he pleaded, "No, *por favor*, no."

Tears started dripping down his cheeks, but it did nothing for me. My mom's abusive boyfriends had beaten whatever goodness and empathy I had out of me a long time ago. "Trey, come over here and hold him steady."

The man started to thrash around. "No! No, no, no!"

Trey didn't hesitate. One thing I really liked about my prospect was that he didn't ask questions or get squeamish when it came down to business.

Once Trey had the cartel scum's hand secured on the table, I got my knife in place. "Last chance. Have anything you want to share?"

He groaned in pain. I could see the anguish on his face. He wanted to talk, but he was too scared of Matteo.

The door opened, and I turned to see Dead Man enter. My brows furrowed from the interruption. "This better be good."

He grinned widely. "Oh, it is."

I pulled my knife back as Dead Man walked over to me and handed me a folder. I opened it and started flipping through pictures of a Mexican woman and four young kids, along with a list of addresses. "What am I looking at?"

142

"I dug up the information you wanted on this motherfucker. Found out some interesting information."

Our captive tensed as Dead Man continued, "Turns out that Carlos here has a wife and four kids just outside Mexicali."

A sinister smirk curved my lips as I made eye contact with Carlos. "Oh, really?"

His face hardened as he snarled, "Don't you dare, *puto*. I'll kill you."

I chuckled. "You're not really in the position to be making threats now, are you?"

He started yelling in Spanish as I took out the picture of the woman and held it up so he could see. "She's pretty. Wonder why she's with an ugly motherfucker like you."

His breathing was so labored and fast that I could hear it from where I was standing several feet away. I took out the picture of four children playing outside, and his eyes went wide.

"How far did you say this was, brother?"

Dead Man shrugged. "About a four-hour ride, give or take."

"So we could have the prospect go pick them up in the van and have them back here by tonight?" I asked, trying to get Carlos to break.

Dead Man smiled. "Definitely."

I read the first address aloud. "Put that in your GPS, prospect, and go pick them up."

Trey took his phone out of his pocket and started tapping the screen.

"No, please, don't. Not *mi hijos*," Carlos begged.

"Then tell me what I want to know," I growled, slamming the file folder down on the table.

He started sobbing, shaking his head.

I snapped my fingers at Trey. "Go get the van from the shop and go pick them up. I want them here before sundown."

"Got it, boss," Trey responded as he started to jog away.

"Wait!" Carlos yelled, his voice breaking into a shrill sob at the end.

Trey stopped, looking at me expectantly. I held up my hand as I locked eyes with Carlos, waiting for him to talk.

Carlos sighed, then closed his eyes and tipped his head back, praying in Spanish. When he opened them again, he said, "The *mujer* we're looking for is named Dixyn Knox."

Fuck. I put on my poker face, trying not to let my anger show. "What for?"

He didn't answer for a few seconds, then exhaled a heavy breath. "She belongs to Matteo. Ran away a couple of months ago, and he wants her back. We heard she was here."

I could feel my nails digging into the skin of my palms. "Yeah, well sounds like she doesn't want him."

He shrugged. "Doesn't matter. El Jefe gets what he wants at any cost."

I'd be damned if they were going to take Dixyn back to some power-hungry cartel lord. I walked away, processing the information I'd just learned. Was she worth starting a war over?

I gestured to Dead Man to follow me to a far corner of the warehouse where Carlos wouldn't hear us. I trusted him the most since he was the one involved and keeping my secret.

"What do you want to do?" he asked.

"I don't know." I exhaled a frustrated breath. I definitely didn't want Dixyn in the hands of the cartel, but I also didn't want to risk the club or my brothers by protecting her. They'd had my back for years, and I'd only known Dixyn a few months.

"You care about her?" Dead Man asked.

I hadn't planned on feeling anything for the young, fiery redhead. But somehow, she'd snuck her way into my cold, dead heart and was slowly bringing it back to life. "I do. I know I shouldn't, but I do."

He nodded. "Well, let's figure out a plan."

A small grin curved my lips. I was thankful for his support, but worried our brothers might not feel the same way since she was Apache's daughter. Letting Matteo have her would hit Apache where it hurts, and that would be to our advantage, but the thought made my blood run cold and my chest ache. "We should still keep this between us. One of us needs to be on her at all times; make sure these wetbacks don't find her."

"Okay."

Ideas ran through my head. "We'll set up a rotation. One of us on her and another tailing the cartel." I glanced over at Carlos and frowned. "We need to figure out how to get rid of the scouts in town."

"We could kill 'em." Dead Man shrugged nonchalantly. "We have enough acid to get rid of the evidence. Plus, the sheriff won't care about some missing illegals."

I rubbed my beard, weighing the options. "That would definitely cause retaliation with Matteo. He'd just send more scouts. If we can get them to leave and report back that they didn't find her here, they'd move on to another city. Keep them the hell out of Laughlin and off our turf."

Dead Man gestured to Carlos. "We could use the wife and kids against him. Tell him we'll let him go and leave his family alone as long as he and his buddies get out of Laughlin and tell Matteo what we want."

I nodded. "And if he doesn't, we'll find them and make him regret crossing us."

Dead Man grinned, clapping me on the shoulder. "Sounds like a plan, brother."

We went back over to Carlos to offer him the deal. "I need you to do something for me, and in exchange, I'll let you go and leave your family alone."

He arched a brow but didn't say anything, so I took that as a sign to continue. "This is what you're going to do. Round up your buddies and go back to Matteo. Tell him that you didn't find the girl and you think she's long gone."

His brow furrowed. "Why should I trust you? How do I know that you won't kill me and my family once I do what you say?"

I chuckled, crossing my arms over my chest. "Look, I may be an asshole, but I'm a man of my word. If you don't, then I'll send my prospect to go pick up your family and bring them back here, and we can see how many fingers of theirs I have to cut off before you change your mind."

He frowned, unresponsive for several seconds. Then he sighed. "Fine. I'll do it."

Internally, I was celebrating, but I kept a stone face on the outside. "Good. Don't think about fucking us over, or you will regret it. We'll be watching your every move to make sure you follow through. If you don't, be prepared for the consequences."

I turned to Dead Man and Trey. "Untie him and take him back to where you picked him up. Make sure no one sees you. Then I want you to tail them and make sure he and his buddies leave town."

"On it, boss," Trey replied as he went to work untying Carlos.

I lit a cigarette and took a drag. I was happy I didn't have to get a woman and kids mixed up in our dirty work. And I hoped Carlos kept his end of the bargain so it stayed that way.

My mind went to Dixyn. I needed to ask her about her relationship with Matteo, no matter how much it pissed me off. I needed to know what to expect if shit went south.

Satisfied with how things worked out, I went to the shop to get some work done. When I got there, Cowboy followed me into my office and closed the door behind him.

"What's up?" I asked, wondering what couldn't wait.

"Forsaken are making a big run tonight. A shit ton of guns to their biggest buyer. Thought we could hit them on the road before they reach the drop."

"Who's running?"

"Apache, Raleigh, and Jameson."

Fuck. My mind went to Dixyn and how she would feel if anything happened to her family.

I crossed my arms over my chest. "I'm not sure that's a good idea with all the shit we have going on with Matteo and the cartel. We don't need more heat on our backs."

Cowboy frowned. "It would be a decent haul, and we'd hurt the Forsaken. A win-win."

"As much as I want to hit the Forsaken where it hurts, now is not the time. We still have cartel running around Laughlin with no idea of motive or how long they're sticking around. We're not hurting for guns; we're getting that shipment from the Chinese next week."

Cowboy clenched his fists. "You're letting that girl get to you."

I tensed, angered by his accusation "Be careful what you say next, brother."

My VP and I stared at each other for several heated moments. Then he turned away and stormed out of my office, letting the door slam behind him.

I blew out a breath of frustration. Was I letting my feelings for Dixyn get in the way of business? Would I take the opportunity to hit the Forsaken if I wasn't fucking her?

I told myself I would make the same decision given the circumstances, but I wasn't sure.

Sitting down at my desk, I took out my phone since I hadn't

looked at it since getting to the warehouse. A text from Dixyn greeted me.

Well, speak of the devil.

Kitten: *Can you meet me tonight?*

A small grin tipped my lips. Dixyn was one of the few things in my fucked-up life that made me happy. Plus, meeting her would give me the opportunity I needed to ask her about Matteo.

Me: *Sure, kitten. Where and when?*

Kitten: *Your place?*

Me: *Ok, I'll meet you there at 11*

Kitten: *K :)*

I put my phone away and sighed. Maybe she was making me soft.

My whole life had been filled with anger, pain, and hardship. All I remembered from my childhood was my mom being drunk or high off her ass and being beaten by her or her string of deadbeat boyfriends. No one showed me any kind of love until I met my brothers.

As far as women went, I never allowed myself to get too close. They were a way to satisfy a need, and that was it. Sex and nothing more. If I didn't feel anything for them, I couldn't be hurt. Plus, no drama. I'd had enough of that to last a lifetime.

But Dixyn made me feel things I'd never felt before. She was different from any other woman that I'd met. Most only saw the cut and wanted me just to say they'd been with a biker.

Dixyn didn't care about my title or affiliation. If anything, that was a negative for her. But she didn't expect me to be something I wasn't. She knew what I was and accepted me anyway. Not many women could handle that.

I tried to push Dixyn from my mind and focus on business. I had too much shit going on to waste time thinking about some broad.

I kept busy for the rest of the day with our books and did some work on a couple of cars. Everything was on track, and the only issue out of order was our shit with the cartel. Our new deal was looking very promising and seemed like it was going to be better than our deal with Matteo.

Right after the shop closed, Dead Man came in my office and closed the door behind him. "The wetbacks are leaving tonight. Trey is gonna tail them, and I made sure to remind Carlos about what's at stake before I left."

I was relieved the cartel wouldn't be a problem anymore. "Good. One less thing to worry about. Let's hope they're not as stupid as they look."

Dead Man chuckled. "I'm gonna head to Harlot's and have a few brews. You staying here?"

I looked at the mess of papers on my desk. "Yeah, I have some stuff to finish up here, then I might head over."

"Okay. Catch you later, brother." We bumped fists before he walked out.

When ten forty-five rolled around, I left to meet Dixyn. She was sitting in her Firebird in my driveway, and I couldn't deny that I liked seeing her there.

I parked my bike and hopped off as she got out of her car. "Hey," she greeted with that beautiful smile of hers.

I couldn't help but look her up and down. She was wearing tiny shorts that hugged her ass and a black tank top that made her tits pop. I wanted to fuck her on the hood of her beast of a car. "Hey."

I led her inside, and we went to the kitchen. "You want a beer?"

"Sure," she answered, taking a seat at my dining room table.

I grabbed us both a beer, popped the tops, then sat down across from her. I handed her a bottle before taking a swig of mine. "So how do you know Matteo?"

Dixyn blinked a few times in disbelief then brought her eyes to mine, narrowing them at me. "That's none of your business."

I slammed my hand down on the table, making her jump. "When cartel come snooping around asking about you, it becomes my business. Now, how do you know Matteo?"

Crossing her arms over her chest defensively, she sat back. "He's my ex."

So the scout was telling the truth. "Why is he sending scouts looking for you?"

She went white as a sheet, and I felt bad for yelling at her. Based on her fearful expression, their relationship wasn't a good one. After a few moments, she put a brave face on and shrugged. "I left him. Guess he wants me back."

"Look, this isn't a game. I—"

Interrupting me, she blurted out, "You think I don't know that?"

"Let me finish," I gritted out, irritated by her interruption. "I need to know what we're dealing with here."

Her face softened, and she looked down at the table. She began picking at the label of the beer bottle. "It's not your problem. I don't want to get you involved."

Too late. I reached across the table and softly took one of her hands in mine. "Tell me, kitten."

She avoided my eyes for several seconds before she finally met my gaze. Biting down on her bottom lip, her eyes filled with tears.

Seeing her like that did all sorts of things to me. I wanted to rip Matteo apart for whatever he'd done to her. I rubbed the back of her hand with my thumb. "It's okay, baby. I won't let him hurt you."

After a few seconds of staring at me in silence, Dixyn exhaled a deep sigh. "Matteo and I were together for about a year. A few months into our relationship, he started to be abusive." She took a deep breath before continuing, "At first, I tried to fight back, but he'd just beat me worse." She sniffled, obviously fighting back tears. "I tried to leave a couple of times, and he put me in the hospital."

I'd never been so angry in my entire life. Jaw clenching, I balled my fist in anger, growling, "Motherfucker."

Her grip on my hand tightened. "It just so happened that my grandpa died while Matteo was in Mexico." Tears trickled down her cheeks. "It was like he was saving me by giving me that opportunity to come home."

I felt sick to my stomach at the thought of my fiery phoenix being beaten. "I'm going to kill him," I promised.

She shook her head, wiping her cheeks with her free hand. "No. I don't want you to get hurt."

I chuckled. "I won't."

"He's dangerous, Ford."

I scoffed. "Sweetheart, I know all about Matteo. He ain't half as dangerous as I am. He'll beg me to kill him when I'm done with him."

She took my hand in both of hers, pleading, "Please don't. I couldn't handle it if you got hurt because of me."

Looking away, I didn't say anything. I didn't want to make any promises I couldn't keep.

She squeezed my hand. "Please, Ford."

I glanced back at her, and the puppy dog eyes she was giving me broke my heart. "Fine," I grumbled. "I'll drop it. For now."

Her body visibly relaxed, and she let out a sigh. "Thank you."

I pulled out my cigarettes. "I need a smoke." I offered her the box. "You want one?"

She took one and put it to her lips. I lit the end, then did the same with my own, taking a long drag. "This is some fucked-up shit." I chuckled.

Dixyn laughed while blowing out smoke. "Tell me about it."

I watched her as I took another puff. "You know I'll protect you, right?"

Her eyes locked with mine. "Will you?"

We stared at each other for several seconds. I'd been denying my feelings for Dixyn since the moment we'd met, but the answer that blared in my head spoke clearly. I'd kill for her. I'd risk my life for her. "Yes."

Her eyes watered as she darted them away from mine, putting the cigarette to her lips again and inhaling. She didn't speak until after slowly blowing the smoke out a few seconds later. "What is this, Ford?" She brought her gaze back to mine and gestured between us. "What are we doing?"

I didn't have an answer to that. All I knew was I wanted her and didn't want anyone else to have her. I blew out a breath and tapped the ashes of my cigarette in the ashtray on the table. "I don't know."

She put out her cigarette and crossed her arms over her chest. "Well, I don't want to be one of your groupies, and I don't want you fucking anyone else."

I arched a brow, holding back a laugh. She was so intense sometimes. "Is that so?"

"I'm not kidding, Ford. Last night you said that you claimed me. What does that mean? Are we together? Are we exclusive? What?"

Taking one last drag of my cigarette, I put it out and blew out the smoke. "I don't know, kitten. We can't really go out on the town holding hands now, can we?"

She rolled her eyes. "You're such an asshole."

I chuckled at her. "What? It's the truth, isn't it?"

"So what are we going to do? Just keep doing what we're doing?"

I shrugged. "Why not? Why ruin a good thing?"

She narrowed her eyes at me. "Because I don't want you fucking other chicks."

I laughed. "Is that what's bothering you?"

"Do you want me to fuck other guys?"

Thinking about Dixyn with another man made me want to break something. "No," I gritted out.

A satisfied smirk curved her lips. "Well, why not?"

"Because you're mine," I growled.

"Well, then maybe we should talk about this ... us."

When she put it like that, I could see her point. "Fine." Leaning back in my chair, I crossed my arms over my chest. "Go ahead —talk."

"Look, I don't want to be an old lady. I've already told you that. But I also don't want you fucking other women if we're going to keep doing this."

"I can live with that." I didn't really have a desire for another woman since meeting Dixyn, but I had needs. "But you need to be available when I want you if you don't want me fucking someone else."

"Fine with me." Dixyn looked pleased, like a cat that caught the canary.

I chuckled. "What else, kitten?"

"Well, I think everything needs to remain secret. If anyone knows, we risk being exposed."

"Makes sense." I liked having Dixyn as my dirty little secret, so I had no problem with that.

A smirk curved my lips. I couldn't believe what we were talking about.

Dixyn started smiling also. "What?"

"Nothing, kitten. Just hard to believe we're really talking about this."

She nodded, tucking a strand of hair behind her ear. "Yeah, I guess it is."

"Any other rules?" I teased, giving her a wry grin.

Playfully rolling her eyes, she shook her head. "No."

"Good," I said, standing up. I plucked her out of her chair and tossed her over my shoulder. "Because I'm tired of talking."

CHAPTER 15

Dixyn

A fter talking with Ford, I felt like a weight had been lifted off my shoulders. We were on the same page about our relationship, and even though I hadn't planned on telling him about Matteo, I was happy that I had someone to confide in after dealing with it on my own for so long. The only problem was that I was worried he'd seek vengeance for me.

And even though I didn't really show it, the fact that Matteo's men were looking for me terrified me. I didn't want to go back to him, and if they took me to him, I'd probably never see my family or friends again.

Or Ford.

Since my dad and brothers were gone, I didn't want to be at home by myself, especially if the cartel were looking for me, so I went to Nina's after I left Ford's. We needed to plan Meghan and Hannah's bachelorette party, anyway.

The wedding was still a few months away, but we wanted to plan an amazing party in Las Vegas and needed to make sure we booked everything in advance.

"I think we should definitely book XS at the Wynn. That place is amazing, and they have night pool parties," Nina suggested.

"Ooh, that sounds fun," I agreed.

Nina nodded. "So that could be where we end the night. And during the day, we can go to the spa and have dinner at the Grand Lux in the Venetian."

I snapped my fingers as an idea popped in my head. "And we have to see a show. We should definitely take them to one of those burlesque shows. I think the one at the Flamingo is highly rated."

"Yes, girl, yes. They are going to love it." Nina squealed with glee. "I'm so excited."

"Me too." The last time I went to Vegas was with Matteo, and I'd had a blast. That had been in the beginning of our relationship before he started getting abusive and controlling. "I think we should go up for a whole weekend. Book a suite for the four of us and make a whole girls' weekend out of it."

"I'm down. Let's do it! I'm sure Meghan and Hannah will love the idea."

I clapped excitedly. "I can't wait. We can hang out at the pool, go to shows, have fancy dinners. We have to do the best of the best that Vegas has to offer."

Nina and I planned out the weekend with activities for each day, including what restaurants to eat at and what clubs we'd party at each night.

After jotting down most of the details, we decided to grab some lunch. I was a little shaken about Matteo sending his men after me, so I was on high alert. I knew what to look for when being tailed since Matteo had men following me whenever he wasn't around back in LA.

I didn't notice anything off as we ate or when I drove back to my dad's. And just to be on the safe side, I grabbed one of my dad's handguns that he'd left behind so that I could keep it with me.

I didn't have to work that afternoon, so I just hung out and relaxed, watching Netflix as I looked over more of my college application paperwork.

A few hours into a new series binge, my phone rang, and my stomach knotted in fear when my dad's number popped up on my phone. He never called me, so something bad must have happened if he was. "Hello?"

"Dixie! We need your help!" My father's voice was panicked. "Jameson took a bullet to the leg and can't ride. We need you to come pick him up."

My heart was pounding as fear for my brother took over. "Oh my God, is he going to be okay?"

"Not if you don't hurry up. I'll send you our location."

Then he hung up. My hands were shaking as I got in my car and waited for my dad to text me their location. When it finally came through, I put it in my GPS and took off like a bat out of hell.

They were about an hour outside of Laughlin, and I prayed I would get there in time. My anxiety was eating away at me as I drove alone, especially since my dad didn't give me any details.

My destination was a deserted gas station in the desert. I saw three motorcycles parked haphazardly near the storefront and my brothers and dad on the ground. Jameson was leaning back against the dirty glass of the door.

Quickly parking, I threw open the door and rushed to my brother's side. A bandana was wrapped around his thigh, which was drenched in blood. "What the hell happened?" I exclaimed, fearing for my brother's life.

"Fucking Kings ambushed us," my dad grunted as he and Raleigh hoisted Jameson up, draping his arms around each of their shoulders.

My stomach dropped. Ford wouldn't do that to me, would he? "Are you sure?"

My dad's brows furrowed in anger. "What the fuck you mean am I sure? Yes, I'm fucking sure, now open the car so I can put your brother inside!"

The concern for my brother trumped everything else I was feeling so I did as I was told. I opened the door to the back seat and my dad and Raleigh deposited James inside. "My bike," Jameson gritted out, wincing in pain.

Shaking my head, I hopped in the driver's seat. I knew a biker's motorcycle was sacred, but my brother needed to worry about not bleeding to death in the back of my car.

"Raleigh's going to stay here with it until Hawk gets here with the van. Then they're going to finish the run," my dad answered before closing the back door.

He came up to my window and I rolled it down. "Where are we going?" I asked.

"Follow me. There's a clinic that has a doctor on our payroll."

Of course. "Okay."

"Don't let your brother die," my dad said as he backed away.

No pressure or anything.

My dad and I sped to the clinic, which was in downtown Laughlin. We pulled into the back, where a man in a doctor's coat was waiting for us. At least my dad was prepared.

The doctor helped my dad get Jameson out of the back and into the clinic. I followed them inside as they took my brother to an exam room.

After getting Jameson settled, my dad and I were asked to sit in the waiting room while they performed surgery on Jameson's leg.

Several hours passed before the doctor came back out and told us that Jameson would be okay. The tightness in my chest finally eased for the first time since getting the call from my dad. I blew out a breath of relief. "Thank God."

My dad and the doctor were talking about the surgery and recovery time, but all I could think about was that my brother could've died because of the Suicide Kings.

Anger replaced my fear and concern. I told my dad I was going to head home since we were assured Jameson was going to be okay, but I was really going to confront Ford.

I got in my car, and the iron stench of blood hung in the air. Tears pricked my eyes as my adrenaline finally wore off, and the severity of the situation sank in.

I whipped out my phone and hastily typed a text to Ford.

Me: *We need to meet now*

He quickly replied, which surprised me.

Ford: *Everything OK?*

Me: *No*

Ford: *I'm at my place*

Me: *omw*

I quickly sped to Ford's place, thankful no cops were around to pull me over for breaking multiple traffic laws. When I pulled into the driveway, Ford came outside.

His face was creased with concern as I got out of the car and stormed up to him. "What's wrong, kitten? Are you hurt?"

Shoving at Ford, angry tears streamed down my face. "What the hell, Ford? Why did you put a hit on my family?"

He frowned, his brow furrowing in confusion. "The fuck you talking about? I didn't put a hit on your family."

I scoffed, pushing him again, even though my efforts did nothing. He barely budged. "Oh yeah? Then, why did my brother almost bleed out in my back seat from a bullet from one of your men?"

He crossed his arms over his chest. "I didn't have anything to do with that."

I was beyond furious and knew I wasn't thinking clearly. To me, everything Suicide Kings equaled Ford since he was their president and called the shots. How could he not know what was going on?

I flew at him, my fear and anger overcoming me as I pounded at his thick arms. Sobs escaped me as I thought about my brother unconscious in the hospital bed, his normal golden skin pale from blood loss.

Ford gripped me by the wrists, stopping my assault. "Quit your shit, Dixyn. This wasn't me."

Struggling against him, I screamed, "Let me go!"

"Calm down, kitten. You're working yourself up over nothing."

I tried to wrench myself from his grasp. "Nothing? Nothing? My brother almost died because one of your men shot him!"

Pulling me against him, he wrapped his arms around me. "Shh, baby. It's okay. I'll find out what happened and make sure whoever did it is punished."

My heart was pounding, my chest heaving with ragged breaths and sobs. I started to relax against him, my body drained from the events of the past few hours.

"Well, well, well. What do we have here?"

The air left me, my body tensing in fear as I heard the click of a gun.

"What the hell are you doing here, Apache?" Ford growled, blocking me with his body.

I looked around Ford, my stomach dropping as I saw my dad with a gun pointed at him.

His eyes locked with mine. "I should be asking my traitor daughter the same thing."

A lump formed in my throat as the guilt I'd been burying resurfaced. "Dad, I didn't mean for this to happen. It just did."

My dad's face was contorted with rage. "Shut up! I can't even stand to look at you right now! You're a whore just like your mother."

His words were like a knife to the heart, and I bowed my head in shame.

"Don't fucking talk to her like that or I'll cut your tongue out," Ford threatened, defending me.

"She's my daughter. I can talk to her any way I goddamn well please!" my dad countered.

"Not when I'm around. You will treat her with respect."

My dad scoffed. "Respect is earned. And she lost all my respect by hooking up with the likes of you." He spat on the ground. "Suicide scum."

I saw Ford's hands bunch into fists. "I'd suggest you get off my property before I force you to."

My dad chortled. "You're in no position to be making threats. I'm the one with the gun."

"I don't need a gun to beat your ass, old man."

Anger and sadness built up inside me as they continued to argue until I felt like I was going to explode. "Stop!" I screamed, causing them both to snap their heads toward me. "You're both acting like children!"

They both stared at me in stunned silence, and I just couldn't deal with either of them at that moment. "You know what? Fuck both of you."

Brushing past Ford, I got in my car. Both of them were immature, controlling assholes, and I was done with their bullshit.

I just hoped they didn't kill each other after I left.

I ended up crashing at Nina's for the next few days. I went by my dad's when no one was home to get a bunch of my clothes and other belongings. I didn't want to talk to him or see him, and I was pretty sure he'd told my brothers I was a traitor.

Ford had called and texted me several times, but I ignored him. I was still trying to make sense of what had happened and decide whether I believed him or not.

Ford was a criminal and a jerk, but he wasn't a liar. He told the truth even when I didn't like it, so I wanted to believe him. However, it was hard to believe that his men would act without his authority.

When I got back to Nina's, I tossed my bag on the couch. "Hey," she greeted as she came out of her bedroom.

"Hey."

"Get everything you needed?"

I sighed, plopping down next to my bag on the couch. "For now. I promise I'll be out of your hair in a week or so. I just need to find a decent apartment."

She waved me off. "Don't worry about it. You can crash here for as long as you need."

I gave her a soft smile. "Thanks. You're a great friend."

"Besides, I kinda like having you in my bed," she teased.

I knew she was trying to lighten the mood, so I forced a laugh.

"Hear from your dad or Ford?" Nina asked as she sat next to me.

"Pretty sure I'm dead to my dad now. And Ford has been calling and texting me, but I haven't responded."

"Are you going to?" Nina asked.

I cradled my head in my hands and groaned. "I don't know. One of his men almost killed my brother. How could I forgive that?"

"But he didn't pull the trigger. You said he didn't know about it."

I scoffed. "But how could he not? He's the president. He gives the orders."

Nina pursed her lips, pausing for a moment. "Do you think your dad knows what all his men are doing all the time?"

I blinked a few times, thrown off by her question. "I don't know."

My friend draped her arm around me. "Why don't you talk to Ford and hear him out? Maybe he really didn't know."

I let out another sigh. "You really think so?"

Nina shrugged. "I think it's worth a conversation."

I thought about her words, then nodded. "Okay. I'll talk to him."

Nina smiled, squeezing my shoulders. "Good."

After taking a shower, I debated what to say in my text to Ford. Gnawing on my bottom lip, I typed out and deleted my message several times before finally sending it.

Me: *I'm sorry. Can we meet and talk?*

I didn't expect him to reply right away, if at all. I went about my day, getting ready for work and pretending not to care whether Ford responded even though I did.

Even though I'd basically attacked him and accused him of lying, he'd protected and defended me when my dad had pulled a gun on us. Instead of thanking him, I'd left him with my enraged father, who could've killed him. I was so blinded by anger that I wouldn't listen to him, and I felt like shit for how I'd acted that night.

I just hoped he would give me the chance I didn't give him.

CHAPTER 16

FORD

After Dixyn stormed off and left me with her old man pointing a gun at my face, I prepared myself for the inevitable.

"I didn't have anything to do with the jump," I stated, keeping my eyes on Apache. If he really believed I had my men jump him and put a bullet in his kid's leg, then he had every reason to shoot me. Our long-standing rivalry combined with that was more than enough.

His eyes were narrowed, his death glare reminding me of Dixyn's. Good thing looks couldn't kill. "And why should I believe you?"

He probably wouldn't believe me, but I told him the truth. "Because I wouldn't do that to Dixyn."

We stared each other down for several tense seconds. The sound of sirens filled the air, and a smirk curved my lips. *Saved by the bell.*

"This ain't over," Apache spat. "Once I find out which one of your men put a bullet in my son, they're dead."

He kept his gun trained on me until he backed up to his bike. Hopping on, he holstered his Glock and took off.

Once he was out of sight, I relaxed, rolling the strain out of my shoulders from tensing up.

I lit a cigarette and took a long drag, my mind roaming to Dixyn. After everything we'd been through, I couldn't believe she would think that I'd put a hit on her family. However, her anger was justified if she really believed that. I wanted to check on her and make sure she was okay but decided to give her some time to cool off.

I was a little pissed that she ditched me while her dad was pointing a gun at me, but she'd been through a lot so I could see why she lost her shit. First, her grandpa died, then she gets all tangled up in my bullshit, and now her brother gets shot by a King. Not to mention, I'd just told her Matteo's men were looking for her. She had shit piling on top of shit.

I finished my cigarette and flicked the butt in my driveway, then went back inside. It was almost four in the morning, and after what had just happened, I needed some sleep. I'd talk to the guys the next day about Dixyn's accusations.

I hadn't slept well, thoughts of Dixyn, and my men going behind my back heavy on my mind. I didn't want to think that Cowboy would do the hit without my authorization, but he seemed pretty pissed that I'd declined his proposal.

I headed to the shop as soon as I woke up. "Where's Cowboy?" I asked as I walked in.

One of the prospects answered, "In the back."

I made a beeline for the back room, set on finding out if my VP disobeyed my orders. Feeling eyes tracking me, I snapped, "Get to work!"

Cowboy, AK, and Dead Man were in the back room with some bricks of coke. They all turned to look at me as I entered. "Did you jump the Forsaken on that run?" I gritted out, balling my fists in an attempt to temper my anger.

Cowboy frowned, crossing his arms over his chest as AK and Dead Man watched us with confusion etched on their faces. "So what if I did?"

His disregard for my authority pissed me off more. "I told you not to. Last I checked, I am the president of this club, and my decisions are final."

Cowboy scoffed. "Not when you're letting your dick do the thinking."

I charged him, enraged by his disrespect. I pushed him until his back hit the wall, growling, "Who the fuck do you think you are?"

His hands gripped the opening of my cut as he tried to push back against me. Cowboy was younger but not as strong as me, and combined with my adrenaline, he barely moved me.

"Whoa, whoa, whoa, brothers, calm down," Dead Man said as he tried to pry us apart. "What the fuck is going on?"

Cowboy tried to wrench out of my grasp. "I found out that the Forsaken were making a run night before last and told our pres here about it. Thought it would be a good idea to hurt them and snatch a good load, but Bullet didn't want to. Said it was too risky with the cartel breathing down our necks, but the truth is he's too pussy-whipped by Apache's whore of a daughter."

I let out a roar before I reared my fist back and punched him in the jaw. All I could see was red as I landed punch after punch on my VP.

It took both Dead Man and AK to pull me away. Cowboy spit blood as my men held me back.

"You think you're so fucking smart. Well, your brilliant plan had Apache showing up at my door pointing a gun at my face because one of you fucking shot his kid. It would've been nice to have been prepared for something like that, but you didn't think about that, did you?"

At least he had the decency to look ashamed. "Fuck," he cursed. "I didn't know."

I roughly shrugged out of AK and Dead Man's hold. "Yeah, well I told you it was a fucking bad idea. Now we have a fucking Forsaken in the hospital, and Apache looking for justice. We'll probably have cops snooping around here any minute now." I stalked toward him again, and he took a step back. Pointing a finger in his face, I gritted out, "Don't ever undermine me again. You better clean up the mess you made and keep the heat off the club."

Then I left the room, needing a cigarette and coffee. I poured myself a cup, opting to keep it black, then went outside to smoke.

A few minutes later, Dead Man joined me outside. "Apache really show up at your place last night?"

Nodding, I took a drag. "Sirens scared him away before he could off me."

"Shit."

I took a sip of coffee as he continued, "The redhead know?"

"Yep." I took another drag. "She let me have it right before Apache showed up."

He shook his head with a humorless chuckle. "Damn."

Speaking of the devil, I decided to send her a message.

Me: *You okay?*

I wasn't sure if she'd respond. She was pretty pissed the night before, and I expected to get the silent treatment for a couple of days.

And I was right. I didn't hear from Dixyn for three days and was starting to worry about her. My concern grew when Dead Man came in and closed my office door one morning. "We've gotten word of some wetbacks in Bullhead City."

Great. "Matteo's men?"

"Think so. They haven't moved into Laughlin yet, so can't be sure."

I nodded. "Keep me updated."

"Will do," Dead Man said as he stood. When he reached the door, I added, "Have a prospect follow Dixyn; make sure she's not being tailed by anyone."

"Sure thing, boss," he replied with a nod before walking out of my office.

A few minutes later, Cowboy appeared in my doorway. He leaned against the doorframe. "Got a minute?"

We hadn't spoken since our confrontation, but he'd made sure to keep the cops out of our business and deny any involvement in the shooting. They had no evidence besides the testimony of the Forsaken, and our rivalry was well-known throughout Laughlin, so it was easy for them to dismiss accusations. Plus Jameson was still breathing so murder wasn't on the table.

"Yeah," I answered.

My VP entered my office. "I just wanted to say I'm sorry about the shit with the Forsaken. I didn't think it would blow back on us like it did."

"I told you it would. You should've listened to me."

He nodded. "You're right. I fucked up."

"Don't let it happen again. I don't need my second undermining me."

"Yes, sir." He gave me a playful salute. "We good?"

I stared at him for a few moments before a smirk curved my lips. "Yeah, brother, we're good."

After Cowboy left, my phone pinged with a text. I glanced down at the screen, seeing Dixyn's nickname popping up.

Kitten: *I'm sorry. Can we meet and talk?*

A grin tipped my lips. I didn't want to admit that I missed my fiery redhead, but I did. And my cock did, too. Since she'd taken days to finally respond to me, I decided to make her wait a while before I replied.

It was over an hour before I messaged her back.

Me: *Sure, kitten. My place in an hour*

Kitten: *K*

I got to my place before Dixyn on purpose, wanting to be prepared for whatever she wanted to talk about. Knowing her, we'd probably fight then fuck.

I lit a cigarette as I waited for her on my porch. She arrived a few minutes early, sheepishly walking up to me after parking her car. "Hey," she greeted softly.

She was wearing a pink tank top and shorts that barely covered her ass.

I blew out the smoke I'd just inhaled. "Hey."

We stared at each other for a few moments of awkward silence. I wordlessly offered her my cigarette, which she took and put to her lips.

After a long drag, she handed the cigarette back to me while exhaling the smoke. I took one more puff before putting it out and going for the door. "Let's head inside."

I opened the door for Dixyn and let her go in first. She walked over to my couch and sat down, then rubbed her palms on her thighs.

Taking a seat next to her, I looked at her expectantly. "Is your brother okay?"

Dixyn bit down on her bottom lip and nodded, avoiding my gaze. "Yeah. He lost a lot of blood, but they were able to do a transfusion. He's going to be fine."

"Good," I said, not knowing what else to say. It was an awkward situation to say the least.

"You really didn't know?" Dixyn asked, her head whipping toward me, warm, brown eyes imploring me for answers.

"My VP had come to me earlier that day and told me about the run. He wanted to ambush them, but I told him not to because we have other shit we're dealing with and didn't need the heat." I paused before releasing a sigh. "Obviously, he didn't listen to me."

Her eyes searched mine, seeking the truth in my words. After a few seconds, she seemed satisfied and nodded. "I'm sorry I didn't listen to you." She gnawed on her bottom lip again. "And for my dad. I didn't know he was going to follow me."

Shrugging, I chuckled. "I've gone through worse. No harm done."

"Well, that was some pretty fucked-up shit."

We both laughed. Dixyn was naturally beautiful, but when she smiled, she was more radiant than the fucking sun.

I ran my knuckles down her cheek. "I've missed you, kitten."

Her cheeks flushed pink, making my cock harden. Growling, I crushed her mouth with mine. Dixyn eagerly returned my advance, parting her lips for my tongue to enter.

She maneuvered herself onto my lap without breaking our kiss. Her fingers fumbled with my belt, making quick work of undoing my jeans and taking out my cock.

I moved her shorts and panties to the side as she guided me to her wet pussy and sank down on me. I groaned, and she gasped as I filled her, her tight cunt gripping me for dear life.

"Fuck, kitten, I love this pussy," I growled against her lips.

Dixyn moaned as she bounced up and down on my dick. I raised my hips, meeting her thrust for thrust, our skin slapping loudly with each contact.

Tangling my hand in Dixyn's hair, I wrapped the thick ponytail around my knuckles and tugged on it. She hissed in a combination of pleasure and pain, biting down on my bottom lip.

She ground her hips against me, the friction bringing me closer to coming. Her eyes fluttered closed as she moaned, "I'm going to come."

I smacked her ass, urging her on. "That's right, baby. Come all over this dick."

Gripping her hips, I roughly slammed myself up into her a few more times until we both came.

Dixyn rested her forehead against mine as we both panted to regain our breath. A lazy smile tipped my lips as we both drifted down from our sex high.

I pressed a soft kiss to her lips, then pushed her wild hair out of her face with a grin. She lifted herself off my lap and adjusted her panties and shorts before jogging to the bathroom.

I heard the shower start, then Dixyn popped her head out. "You coming?" she asked with a mischievous smile.

I couldn't help but grin as I got up and joined my woman.

After getting dirtier in the shower, we cleaned up, then I ordered a pizza. Dixyn was wearing one of my shirts, but it was more like a dress on her.

I smiled as she danced around my kitchen to some pop song on the radio, drinking a beer. My heart warmed at the sight, and I realized I couldn't remember a time I'd been that happy. She filled a part of me that always felt like something was missing, and I didn't want to lose that.

The doorbell rang, and I went to greet the pizza delivery guy and pay him. When I brought the pizza to the table, Dixyn turned off the music and sat down.

I grabbed some paper plates and handed them to her before sitting down myself. After we each got a slice, I asked, "Have things been okay at home since your dad caught us?"

She finished chewing her bite, then let out a sigh. "I haven't seen him since. I've been staying at Nina's."

I nodded as I took a bite. "If you need a place to stay, you can crash here."

Her cheeks turned pink as a smile curved her lips. "Oh, yeah? That wouldn't be too much for you?"

I hadn't lived with a woman since my mother. I didn't want things between us to get too serious, but I would worry less if she was staying with me so I could keep an eye on her. The cartel knew better than to come to my house. Not to mention, I'd have pussy on demand. "No. It's partly my fault that this happened, and I own up to my mistakes. Plus, I like seeing you dance around my kitchen in my shirt."

"I'm sure that's the reason you'd want me around," she responded with a playful eye roll.

"Well, I'd be lying if I said that I wouldn't enjoy you in my bed and being able to put my dick in that pussy whenever I want."

She shook her head with a laugh. "I might take you up on that. Not like we have to hide anymore."

I nodded and took another bite of my pizza. My thoughts went to the news Dead Man had told me earlier about the cartel in Bullhead City. Technically, they were out of Laughlin, but still too close for comfort. I hoped that they were smart enough to stay away from Dixyn. "I can protect you better here, too."

Her eyes widened a little as she swallowed deeply. "I feel safest with you."

I swelled with pride. "I'll always protect you, kitten. Never doubt that."

She looked down, biting back a sob. "I don't want them to take me back to him, Ford. Please don't let them take me back."

Getting out of my seat, I went over to her and knelt down. Tears were trickling down her cheeks, and my chest tightened. I hated seeing her scared and upset, and I cursed Matteo for hurting her. "Hey, I'm not going to let them touch you." I lifted her chin so I could look her in the eyes. "I will end anyone who tries to hurt you, you hear me?"

Nodding, she threw her arms around my neck, squeezing me tightly. I wrapped her in my embrace, sitting in the chair as I pulled her into my lap. "I won't let anything happen to you, kitten." I pressed a kiss to her temple.

Having her in my arms was the best feeling. There was no denying Dixyn meant something to me, but every time I tried to voice how I felt, I couldn't. Fear and doubt strangled the words in my throat. Letting her in meant being vulnerable, and being vulnerable meant I could get hurt. I didn't need anyone, especially the cartel, knowing my weakness.

I only had one, and it was her.

CHAPTER 17

Dixyn

Even though I hadn't wanted my father to find out about Ford and me, I was happy that it had brought us closer together.

I decided to take him up on his offer for the time being, until the issue with Matteo was resolved. I only felt safe with Ford and felt like I couldn't rely on my family to protect me anymore after my dad had labeled me a traitor. Not to mention I didn't want to put Nina in danger by being there.

I still planned to get my own apartment soon, but it made sense to stay with Ford with the cartel still lurking around. He was the only one capable of protecting me.

After my small breakdown, Ford made love to me and I'd fallen asleep in his arms. After our night at Spirit Mountain, there was so much more emotion involved when we had sex, and our connection deepened each time.

We never talked about our feelings, though. We avoided it, wanting to pretend things weren't serious between us when it was obvious they were. We were both seriously fucked up, but somehow, we still worked.

When Ford left to go to the shop, I went over to Nina's to get my things and finish planning the bachelorette party since it was only a couple of weekends away.

Once we started calling and making reservations, I wondered how we were going to pay for everything. "Nina, how are we going to get the money for all this?"

A mischievous smirk curved her lips. "Don't you worry about that. I'll take care of it."

I was a little taken aback. We worked the same job, so I knew the kind of money she made. I crossed my arms over my chest, arching a brow. "What aren't you telling me?"

Rolling her eyes, she sighed. "I'm not going to get out of this, am I?"

I chuckled, thinking back to the time the girls had forced me to tell them about Ford. "No. Now spill."

Nina bit down on her bottom lip nervously. "I kinda have a sugar daddy."

"What?" I exclaimed, not sure I just heard what I thought I heard.

She laughed. "Okay, that sounded bad. It's not like that."

"Explain," I urged, hoping my friend wasn't whoring herself out for money.

"Well, after your caveman biker forced you to leave the poker game that night, I hit it off with one of the city councilmen. We'd been flirting the whole night, and once the game ended, he made a point to find me."

I couldn't believe she hadn't told me. "And?"

"And he wanted to see me again. We've gone out a few times since, and I really like him, Dee."

I smiled. "But?"

"But he's forty-three. And I'm just scared that ..." she trailed off, not finishing her sentence.

"Scared of what, Nina?"

Her eyes met mine, and I'd never seen her look so unsure. "That I'm not good enough."

I frowned. "What the hell are you talking about? Has this guy been putting you down or telling you shit?"

"No. No, it's not like that." She shook her head, then sighed dreamily. "He's amazing. He wants to take things further, but I'm scared. I mean he's an important man, and I'm just a casino waitress. He lives in a mansion on the river, and I live in this shit apartment."

I reached out my hand and placed it over hers. "Nina, you're amazing, too. Titles and money aren't the only things that determine a person's worth. He's lucky to have someone like you. You're kind, passionate, and beautiful. You help others even though you don't have much, and you speak your mind."

She nodded, sitting up straighter. "Yeah, you're right. I just don't want to mess this up, you know? He's a really great man. And he's amazing in bed."

"If there's one thing I've learned in life, it's not to let fear hold you back from what you want. You'll end up regretting it for the rest of your life."

Nina wrapped me in a hug. "Thank you. I really needed to hear all this."

When I pulled back, I smiled. "Anytime. Now, you still didn't explain the whole sugar daddy thing."

She laughed. "Well, he added me as an authorized user on his black card. And it has no limit."

I gaped at her. "Oh my God, Nina. Holy fucking shit."

"Yeah, and I told him about the bachelorette party, and he told me to have fun and spare no expense."

I chuckled. "Damn, girl, you hit the jackpot. Literally."

"It's really not about the money. I would still want him regardless. If anything, I feel like the money gets in the way."

"Well, don't let it. Consider it icing on your favorite cake. It's hard to find rich men who aren't stuck-up assholes. I think you should tell him how you feel."

Nina nodded with a wistful smile on her face. "I think I will. He's taking me to dinner tonight. I'll tell him then."

"Good." I clapped my hands, then let out a little squeal. "I'm so happy for you, girl." She deserved happiness more than anyone I knew.

We finalized the remaining plans for the bachelorette party, then I got ready to go back to Ford's.

"You sure you're okay over there? I don't mind you staying here," Nina commented as she walked me to the door.

I smiled. I didn't have any doubts about staying with Ford. I felt like I was where I was supposed to be. "I'm good, girl. Don't worry about me."

My friend hugged me. "Okay. Tell Ford that if he hurts you, he has to answer to me."

I laughed. "I'll be sure to let him know."

I decided to make Ford dinner that night to thank him for letting me stay at his place. I stopped by the grocery store on my way there and noticed a biker seemed to be following me as I shopped. I wondered if my dad had sent someone after me, so I grabbed a meat tenderizer to defend myself in case something happened.

After gathering everything I needed to make dinner, I was sure I was being followed, and fear crept in my stomach. I knew my dad was pissed off at me, but I never thought he'd send someone to hurt me.

Anger overcame my fear, giving me a sudden bout of courage. Tenderizer in hand, I approached the biker and confronted him, "Why are you following me? Did my dad send you?"

The biker looked shocked and a little fearful. I raised my weapon, attempting to show I meant business.

He put up his hands in a gesture of surrender. "Wait, wait, wait.

I'm not here to hurt you. Bullet sent me to make sure you were okay; make sure the cartel aren't following you."

My brow furrowed as my mind put two and two together. "Oh." I lowered the meat tenderizer. "Sorry about that."

The biker gave me a sheepish grin. He looked young, maybe around my age or a few years older. Probably a prospect if Ford put him on babysitting duty. "Name's Trey."

I felt slightly embarrassed for almost attacking him with a kitchen tool. "Dixyn. Sorry again."

"No harm done." He ran a hand over his buzzed head. "I'll try to be more stealthy. Obviously, I need some work."

I laughed, then went back to my cart and checked out.

When I got back to Ford's, I started on dinner. I planned to make him a nice pork tenderloin with risotto and honey glazed carrots.

I sent him a text as the pork was in the oven.

Me: *What time will you be home?*

He replied right away.

Ford: *Why? Miss me?*

I couldn't help but smile and roll my eyes as I messaged him back.

Me: *I have a surprise for you*

His response was almost instant.

Ford: *Be there in 20*

Me: *Perfect*

Twenty minutes was just the right amount of time to finish everything. I was putting our plates on the table and opening a bottle of wine as Ford walked in. Seeing him still gave me butterflies. "Hi," I greeted with a smile.

The surprised grin on Ford's face was priceless as he looked from me to the table and back. "What's all this?"

I set the bottle of wine down and walked over to him. "I wanted to make you a nice dinner for letting me stay here."

He pulled me against him, pressing a scorching kiss on my lips. "Kitten, if you keep doing shit like this, you can stay as long as you want."

Giggling, I led him to the table and poured us each a glass of wine. I wasn't sure if Ford drank wine, but I wanted our dinner to be romantic and classy, and beer just didn't fit that equation.

I handed Ford a glass as I took a sip of my own. The way he was looking at me made my sex clench, like he wanted to devour me instead of the meal I'd just made.

Ford set the glass down and picked me up, propping me up on the table. Then he got down on his knees and pushed my dress up.

"What are you doing?" I asked.

His hands snaked up my thighs and pulled my panties down. "I want dessert first."

"But the food will get cold," I pointed out, but Ford wasn't hearing it. And as soon as he buried his face in my sex, my protest died on my lips.

As we lay in bed after having dinner then having sex, Ford played with my hair. I let out a sigh of content as I rested my head on his chest.

He pressed a kiss on the top of my head. "That food was delicious, babe."

A smile curved my lips. "Oh, yeah? What was your favorite part?"

His chest rumbled with a soft chuckle. "Your pussy."

I laughed, craning my neck to look up at him. Tugging on his long beard, I pulled his lips to mine and kissed him. "You can have seconds if you'd like."

"I think I'll take you up on that." He tucked some hair behind my ear. "My prospect told me you almost killed him today."

I scoffed playfully. "I did not. I was just protecting myself. I didn't hurt him."

Ford kissed my forehead. "I know. I'm glad you did. I like that you're aware of your surroundings and aren't afraid to defend yourself."

"You could've let me know you had someone following me. I thought my dad sent someone after me."

Ford's face hardened into a frown. "He'd be a dead man if he did."

Even though I was happy with Ford, I hated that I'd lost my family because of it. "Do you think he'll forgive me one day?"

His features softened. "I don't know, kitten. Bikers are stubborn assholes when it comes to their clubs and respect. What we're doing is a total slap in the face to the Forsaken."

I sighed. "But I'm not in the club. I don't care about all the politics."

Ford chuckled. "Whether you like it or not, you were a part of the club as soon as you were born. You have Apache's blood in your veins, and that makes you Forsaken."

I huffed, exasperated by the situation. Fucking bikers.

Ford shifted beneath me, moving me off his sculpted body and sliding down between my thighs. "Now, about those seconds ..."

~

The next couple of weeks were almost perfect. Ford and I were getting used to living together and had arguments here and there, but they always led to makeup sex not long after. I loved falling asleep in his arms and waking up with his erection pressing against my ass.

The morning that the girls and I were planning to leave to Vegas, Ford didn't want to let me out of bed, holding me tightly in his arms. "Baby, I have to get ready." I chuckled, trying to squirm out of his embrace. He'd already distracted me twice with sex to keep me in bed.

He sighed, letting me go. "Fine." When I got out of bed, he smacked my ass, and I couldn't help but giggle. My biker was insatiable.

When I finished getting ready, Ford walked me out to my car and loaded my bags. When he finished, he caged me between his arms against the car. "Be careful. Matteo's men may still be looking for you."

Chuckling, I gripped his cut and pressed a soft kiss to his lips. We hadn't heard much about the cartel in the last week or so, and the last we'd heard, they were in Bullhead City. "You really think they'd try to kidnap me in Vegas? There are too many people to kidnap someone without being noticed."

He grunted. "Yeah, well make sure to stick to the crowds. I'm gonna have Deuce and Trey follow you just to be safe."

I groaned. "I'll be fine. You don't have to do that." I thought it was sweet that he was worried about me, but I didn't want two bikers following the girls and me all around Vegas. Trey following me around Laughlin was bad enough.

Tucking a strand of hair behind my ear, he kissed my forehead.

"Well, I'm going to. I don't want anything happening to you when I'm not around."

I couldn't help but smile as my stomach fluttered. "Okay, old man."

He captured my mouth with his, kissing me so fucking good that I could barely see straight when he was finished. "Now, get out of here before I take you back in the house and not let you out of bed."

Giggling, I bit down on my bottom lip. I almost wanted to take him up on his offer, but Nina and I had organized everything, and I needed to be there. Plus, I needed some girl time after shacking up with my biker for the last two weeks. "Keep it warm for me. I'll be back in it Sunday night."

He grinned down at me. "You better."

After several more minutes of making out and lots of heavy groping, I finally got in the car and drove to Hannah and Meghan's. The sun had barely risen when I arrived, and Nina was already there.

I knocked on the door, and the three of them greeted me with huge smiles and voices too loud for that early in the morning. "Dee!" They all squealed before pulling me in for a group hug.

"Are you ready to get this party started?" Nina asked when they let me go.

She had what I was pretty sure was a mimosa in her hand. "Are you drunk already?"

"Girl, I plan to be drunk all weekend."

I chuckled, and Hannah shook her head with a laugh. "Want some coffee?"

"Yes, please." Since I'd stayed up all night with Ford having sex and slept maybe three hours, fatigue was finally catching up to me. Sometimes I wondered who was the older person in our relationship because he gave me a run for my money.

I set my bags by the door, then followed Hannah to the kitchen. "Did y'all get any sleep?"

She poured me a steaming mug. "A couple of hours. We were both too excited, especially since you won't give us any details."

I giggled as she handed me the mug. "It wouldn't be a surprise if we told you."

She scoffed playfully. "Whatever." Pouring another mug, she called out, "Nina, get your ass in here and drink this!"

Nina bounced in, drunken bliss on her face. "Yes, ma'am."

After we all finished our coffee, we loaded up Meghan's SUV and started the hour and a half drive to Vegas. I noticed the two motorcycles following us, but the others didn't seem to.

Our mini road trip was filled with laughter, off-key singing, and playful banter between the four of us. We'd booked a suite at the Wynn and opted for early check-in so that we didn't have to wait around with our luggage all day.

To say the suite was amazing would've been an understatement. Decorated in hues of cream and gold with marble floors, plush carpet, and high-end furniture, it was nicer than most of the homes I'd been in.

"Oh. My. God." Hannah gasped. "This is just wow, you guys."

We all gaped in awe as we took in the suite. The bathrooms had rain showers and infinity-edge bathtubs and both bedrooms had a balcony overlooking the Strip.

"Holy shit," Meghan commented. "This place is unreal."

After taking everything in, we put our luggage in our rooms, changed into our bathing suits, then went to have a poolside brunch at one of the hotel's restaurants.

After we ordered, Meghan beamed at us. "I can't believe you two planned all this for us. This is already amazing, and we just got here."

Happiness and pride buzzed within me. "You deserve it."

Nina raised her mimosa. "To the best bachelorette weekend."

"And the best friends a girl can have," I added, raising my bellini.

We clinked our glasses, then finished brunch before heading down to the neighboring pool. The first day was planned to be a lazy, relaxing day, mainly hanging out at the pool and gearing up for the weekend. We'd planned to see the burlesque show that night, also.

After a few hours at the pool, Meghan and I decided to go upstairs and take a nap to prepare for the long night ahead while Nina and Hannah opted to stay at the pool.

As Meghan and I were in the elevator, she asked, "So, how's everything with your forbidden biker?"

My lips curved up. "Really good, actually. Better than I ever expected, honestly."

She smiled at me. "Good. You deserve the best, Dee. Are you planning to fully move in?"

Thinking about taking things to that level with Ford made my stomach knot. Things were going good the way they were, and I didn't want to mess that up. "No. I've been looking for an apartment, and I plan to move out by the end of next month. I want to have my own place before I start school in the fall."

"That's good. Don't want to rush into a commitment too fast."

I nodded. "Exactly."

After napping for about two hours, I felt refreshed. Nina and Hannah had come back up sometime while I was asleep, and we all started getting ready for our first night in Vegas.

As we walked the Strip that night after the burlesque show, the girls and I chatted and laughed.

"That was amazing," Hannah gushed.

"The girls were so hot," Meghan agreed, fanning herself.

"They were pretty hot," Nina seconded.

I giggled as we walked. I noticed Ford's men trailing a good distance behind us. Shaking my head, I rolled my eyes but couldn't help but smile. Ford's concern for me made my stomach flutter, and I felt safer with his prospects following me.

I just hoped they didn't report back everything I did to Ford because I planned to get a little wild with my girls.

Our last night in Vegas, we were at the pool area of the XS nightclub at the Wynn. We'd bought a bottle of champagne and each raised a flute to clink them together. "To Vegas, baby!" Nina toasted.

"Woo!" I cheered before downing my drink.

Hannah refilled my glass. "Let's make this last night count!"

We'd had such a blast. Everything had gone according to plan and exceeded our expectations. All the dinners were amazing, the shows and clubs were above and beyond fun, and there was no shortage of laughter and smiles. It would definitely be a weekend to remember, and I'd had the time of my life with my friends.

Music and multicolored strobe lights pulsed in the air as people danced around in bathing suits. The pool was filled with loungers, foam noodles and inflatable pool toys that partygoers were tossing around in the water.

"You guys want to get in?" I asked, gesturing to the pool.

"Hell yeah," Nina said.

We had booked a VIP area for the night, so we left our bottle and headed to the water with glasses in hand.

People were dancing in the shallow end of the pool, and I loved the vibe of the night. It seemed like it was going to be a perfect end to our girls' weekend.

The entire pool area was packed, but I could see Ford's prospects hanging out by the bar. I wondered how they managed to get access to all the places we went, but I knew bikers had a way of getting what they wanted, whether it was with money or by force.

After a few more drinks, I needed to go to the bathroom.

"I gotta use the ladies' room," I announced in a drunken squeal. "I'll be right back."

My friends were hitting a beach ball back and forth to each other. "Okay," they called out in a chorus of girly giggles.

I grabbed a towel from the towel station and wrapped it around myself before squeezing through the crowd to get to the bathroom.

After relieving my very full bladder and washing my hands, I emerged from the bathroom to promptly smack into a broad chest. "Whoops, sorry," I apologized with a drunken giggle.

I moved around the man only to have another step in front of me. "Excuse me," I scoffed, my buzz fading from the jerks purposely getting in my way.

When I noticed the presence of the other two men closing in around me, I knew I was in trouble. I felt the cold press of metal against my bare back and stiffened.

The man in front of me smirked. "Hello, Dixyn." He had a thick Spanish accent, and my stomach dropped. "Matteo has been looking for you."

CHAPTER 18

FORD

I hadn't heard from Dixyn since the morning, and worry was eating away at me. I didn't want to be the controlling, overprotective boyfriend, but I couldn't help it when the cartel were involved. Deuce and Trey were giving me updates every few hours, but I was still uneasy. I was glad she was having a good time, but I wanted her back in my bed already.

My phone rang, and Deuce's number displayed on the screen as I was playing poker with the guys at the shop. A lump formed in my throat as dread came over me. We'd been communicating via text the whole trip, so it was strange for him to be calling. "Yeah?" I answered.

He didn't answer for a few seconds, and that only intensified my concern. "The cartel got Dixyn," he finally said.

My stomach dropped as my worst fear was confirmed. "What?" I gritted out, my voice low and lethal.

The laughter and talk around the poker table stopped as my brothers sensed the change in my demeanor.

My prospect's voice was shaky as he responded, "Matteo's guys. They took her from a club in Vegas. We couldn't stop them—there were too many people. Trey's following them now." His words were rushed and frantic.

Dammit, I told Dixyn to be careful. And I had my prospects follow her and her friends to be safe. *This can't be happening.* I felt sick to my stomach. A few moments of silence passed as my mind raced, my pulse thrumming in my ears. "I told you to fucking watch her!" I yelled into the phone before chucking it against the wall. Rage and fear overcame me, and I roared, flipping over the table, then punching a hole in the wall closest to me. Chips and cards scattered all over the floor as everyone at the table stood.

I clenched my fists as I tried to calm myself down, but it was hard when all I could think about was what the cartel would do to Dixyn once they got her wherever they were going. My heart was pounding with fear and adrenaline.

"Calm down, brother," Cowboy said, placing a hand on my shoulder.

Shrugging him off, I growled, "Don't tell me to fucking calm down! The cartel have my woman."

Cowboy held his hands up, palms facing me. "We'll find her. We just have to come up with a plan."

Desperation was creeping through my veins as I tried to figure out what to do. "Call Trey," I barked at Kojack. "Find out where they're going." I turned to AK. "Get every damn piece we have and get all the brothers here now."

I stalked toward the door as Cowboy called out, "Where are you going?"

"To get backup." I couldn't believe what I was doing, but I was fucking desperate.

Ten minutes later, I pulled up outside Apache's strip club and parked my bike. Two guys in Forsaken cuts were outside and stood at attention when they noticed me.

As I approached them, one asked, "You lost?"

I hadn't seen Apache since the night he'd come to my house and threatened me with a gun. "I need to speak with Apache. Now."

They both looked at each other and chuckled. "I don't think you're in the position to be making demands."

I didn't have time for their shit. Dixyn was in trouble, and she needed me. I grabbed the asshole closest to me and pushed him up against the wall, my knife to his throat. I glared at the other one. "Get Apache before I spill his blood all over this concrete."

The guy held up his hands. "Be cool, man. I'll get him."

I pulled my X9 out as I waited for Apache, keeping my knife steady on the other biker's neck.

As the door opened, I pointed my gun at it, ready for anything. Apache came out with his sons, eyes narrowed angrily as Raleigh and Jameson pointed their guns at me. "What the fuck are you doing here, Bullet?" Apache spat.

"I need to talk to you."

He crossed his arms over his chest, eyes darting between me and his man I had my knife against. "Well, go ahead, talk."

"The cartel took Dixyn."

His arms dropped. "What?"

I pulled my knife from his man's throat and held up my hands in a gesture of peace. Apache motioned to his sons to put their guns down, then turned back to me as I said, "One of my guys is tailing them right now. I'm going after her. I came here to see if we could put our bullshit aside and work together to get her back."

"How do we know what you're saying is true?" Jameson questioned. "How do we know this isn't some bullshit trick?"

"Look, kid, I don't give a shit if you believe me or not. I'm going after Dixyn with or without you. Just thought I'd let you know."

I turned to go back to my bike, pissed at myself for wasting time. I needed to get to Dixyn before they crossed the border, or else it would infinitely harder to find her.

"Wait," Apache called after me.

I stopped at my bike as he approached. "We'll come with you. All of my men and weapons are at your disposal." He stuck his hand out. "Let's go get my little girl."

~

I went back to the shop after making plans to meet up with the Forsaken after we prepared. Our entire arsenal was laid out on the poker tables in the back room. "Is this all of it?" I asked AK.

"Everything; even our personal stock."

We had enough for a small army, and it still might not be enough to take on the cartel, but that wasn't going to stop me. I clapped him on the shoulder. "Good."

Kojack came up to me. "Trey said they're on fifteen heading south. He doesn't think he's been spotted yet."

"Think they're heading to Tijuana?" Cowboy asked.

"Not yet. They probably need to figure out how they're going to smuggle Dixyn in first."

I hope.

"We need to have a meeting. Now," I said, heading toward our meeting room. Once all my brothers were in their respective seats, I continued, "I know most of you don't approve of my relationship with Dixyn, so there will be no hard feelings if you don't want to come. I would love to have all my brothers by my side, but I understand that this isn't your fight."

No one said anything for a few seconds before AK spoke, "Your fight is our fight. I'm with you no matter what, brother."

"Me, too," Cowboy stated.

All my brothers spoke their agreement, and pride swelled within me. Then my gut twisted as I thought about telling them about my deal with Apache. "You should know that the Forsaken are going, too. I reached out to Apache since he has an invested interest in this, and we could use all the help we can get if we're going to war with the cartel."

You could hear a pin drop in the silence that followed my statement. I suspected a few men might change their minds with the bomb I'd dropped.

"Damn, you must really love her," Cowboy commented.

I hadn't said the words to her or admitted it out loud, but there was no denying it. I was willing to go to war with the cartel and seek out our biggest rival's help for Dixyn. "Yeah, I do."

"Then we're with you, brother," my VP stated.

I looked around to all the faces of my brothers, who all nodded at me. "Let's go rescue my old lady."

We met up with the Forsaken at a rest stop a few miles outside of Laughlin. Things were tense to say the least, but the men were being civil for their presidents' sake.

Kojack shoved his phone in his pocket and came over to me. "Just talked to Trey. He said they're still on fifteen just passing the Mojave Preserve."

I nodded. "It's about five and half hours from Vegas to Tijuana without stopping." I pointed at the map laid out on a picnic table in front of us. "If they're on fifteen, they're probably going to take that all the way down."

"Think they'll stop on the way?" Raleigh asked.

I shook my head. "Doubt it. They probably won't risk it. They know I'll be coming for her."

"We have to stop them before they get to Mexico. If they get her across the border, it'll be ten times harder to get her back," Apache said.

I nodded. "I know."

We knew the location and layout of his compound. With the men we had we could definitely infiltrate it, but there would be a lot of bloodshed.

We all stared at the map for several seconds before I pointed again. My mind raced as I tried to figure out the best plan. Dixyn needed me, and I'd promised her that Matteo would never hurt her again. I didn't want to let her down.

I traced my finger on the map. "Let's plan to take the forty to fifteen and intercept them there. Run them off the road, block them, blow out their tires, whatever we need to do to stop them."

Everyone nodded or grunted their approval, and we all mounted our bikes and got on the forty toward fifteen. I called Trey on the way, and if we hauled ass, we could hit them at the intersection of the two highways.

I just prayed we made it in time.

We were a few miles outside of where the forty intersected the fifteen when Trey called. I pressed the Bluetooth in my ear and answered, "Hello?"

"Are you close? Because something is going down right now."

"The fuck you mean?" I asked, my concern for Dixyn growing.

"They pulled off the highway just past the forty and another crew in a different SUV just pulled up behind them."

My mind raced as I tried to figure out what they were doing. Then it hit me. "Shit, they're probably going to transfer her to the other vehicle and transport her over the border in that. We need to stop them before they complete the transfer."

"What do you want me to do, boss?"

"If they start to leave, create a diversion. Blow out their tires, kill someone, I don't care just don't let them leave. We'll be there in less than five."

When the SUVs came into view, my heart started to pound. Dixyn was so close. I didn't want to put her in any more danger than she already was in, but I didn't see any way around bullets being exchanged.

I motioned to everyone behind me to be ready. We didn't know exactly how things would go down, but I'd do anything to get Dixyn.

We were lucky to be coming from behind because we had a small element of surprise, but it was hard to ignore the rumble of the engines of over thirty bikes.

I heard gunshots and the sound of bullets whizzing past me as we neared. Pulling out my X9, I quickly scanned for Dixyn before returning fire. Chaos ensued as my men shot at the two SUVs and the Forsaken went to block them off.

Then a man pulled Dixyn out of the back of one of the SUVs and I froze, stopping my bike. I held up my fist, signaling my men to cease fire. "Stop!" I bellowed over all the noise.

The Forsaken were in position, and all my men had their weapons trained on the cartel. We had them outnumbered three to one, but the gun pressed against Dixyn's temple tipped the scales.

Her eyes met mine, and she tried to escape her captor's grasp. "Ford," she cried out, the strangled sound piercing my heart. I had to stop myself from going to her, a growl rumbling low in my throat.

She was wrapped in only a towel, and her hair was in a messy bun on the top of her head. She looked terrified, and I wanted to personally torture every motherfucker there for touching her.

The man with the gun to her head addressed me. "Let us go or I kill her."

I thought he was bluffing. I doubted Matteo wanted to kill Dixyn. Otherwise, she'd be dead already. "I don't think your boss will like it if she ends up dead."

The cartel scum scowled, pressing the gun harder against Dixyn's temple, and I tensed. "If he can't have her, he doesn't want anyone to have her. He said to bring her back dead or alive."

Well, shit.

I glanced over at Apache, who gave me a stiff nod. Even though I didn't want to let Dixyn go, it was better for us to regroup, then go after her. There was too much risk for her to get hurt in the massacre that would occur if shit went down.

I nodded back, then turned my attention back to the cartel asshole. "Fine." I held my hands up. "We'll let you go."

He sneered. "If I see one motorcycle following us, I put a bullet in her head; got it?"

The fear in Dixyn's eyes almost broke me. I hoped she knew I was going to come for her. "Yeah, I got it."

Keeping my eyes on hers, I watched as he put her in the back of the other SUV and got in behind her. Then the rest of the men got in the two vehicles and drove off.

When they were out of sight, I cursed, "Fuck!"

The Forsaken regrouped with my men on the side of the road. "What are we going to do?" Raleigh asked, panic evident in his frantic tone.

"Trey, go after them, but stay out of sight." I grabbed him by his cut and pulled him to me, getting in his face. "I swear to God if they see you and kill her because of it, I will slit your fucking throat. You hear me?"

His Adam's apple bobbed as he swallowed deeply. "Yes, sir."

I shoved him away. "Good. Now, hurry up before you lose them."

Once Trey was gone, I addressed the group. "Since that plan went to shit, we have to move to plan B. We're going to have to attack Matteo's compound."

I took the file I had on Matteo out of my saddlebag and smoothed it out over the seat of my bike. "He has guard towers on each corner of the property. We'll have to take them out quickly and quietly." I glanced at Apache. "You have a good sniper?"

"Yeah, Hawk. Best long-range marksman I've ever seen."

"Okay." I looked back down at the blueprint of Matteo's compound. "I think the best plan would be for us to split up. One club take the front of the property, the other take the back. Have snipers take out all the guard towers, then try to sneak in without drawing any attention."

Apache nodded. "And if we do draw attention?"

"We rain down hell on them," I answered. I was willing to go to any lengths to get Dixyn back.

Matteo's compound was a couple of hours from the border outside Tijuana. Based on the images we had of the layout, there was a small patch of trees right outside the property we could use to conceal ourselves before attacking. We made plans to use that as our regrouping point.

We were still a couple of hours from the border, so we set out on our way, only stopping to refill our tanks with gas. Trey had tracked the vehicles to an abandoned convenience store, but they were already gone when he got there. After searching the place, he informed me of a man-made tunnel at the back of the store, so we planned to use that to cross into Mexico.

Once we arrived at the store, I surveyed the inside. The tunnel was pretty tight, and the only way we were going to get the bikes through was to walk them. And there was no way in hell I was leaving my bike behind.

We used a couple of old steel doors that had fallen off the hinges as a ramp for us to wheel the bikes down, then we carefully made our way through the tunnel. It was a tight squeeze to say the least, especially for a bunch of burly bikers.

"Hey, Dimes, bet you haven't been in something this tight since you popped that virgin's cherry at Harlot's a few years back," Ajax teased.

The guys laughed and oohed as Dimes retorted, "Hey, fuck you, man. Every bitch I bang is tighter than your momma's pussy."

The guys kept trading jabs and jokes back and forth, but all I could think about was getting to Dixyn. I didn't want Matteo putting his hands on her again, and I'd promised I wouldn't let him hurt her. I felt like the biggest piece of shit for not keeping my promise.

But I sure as hell was going to make it up to her, burning Matteo's place to the ground in the process.

CHAPTER 19

Dixyn

After the confrontation with the bikers, I had hope that I was going to be saved. Even though Ford had let them take me, the look in his eyes told me he was going to come for me and was going to kill anyone that got in his way.

I just hoped he didn't get himself killed in the process.

The men in the SUV with me spoke in Spanish for most of the trip so I didn't understand what they were saying. I had a feeling we were going to Mexico, which scared the shit out of me. I knew that most of the people they took over the border to Matteo's compound were never found again.

But I had faith in Ford. I needed to in order to keep from losing my shit.

We stopped outside an abandoned convenience store somewhere in the desert. Light flooded in as the back of the SUV opened and one of the men grabbed me by my arm and hauled me out.

I tried to wrench from his grasp. I hated being manhandled, and it triggered my defense mechanisms. Gripping me tighter, he led me into the run-down shop.

At the back of the store, the floor was covered with cardboard, pieces of wood, and old, dirty rugs. Two of the men moved the coverings aside to reveal a hole in the floor. They were all speaking in Spanish again as they started to jump down into the hole one by one.

Another man approached me, shoving clothes at me. "Change," he ordered.

I frowned at him, gripping my towel tighter. "I'm not changing in front of all of you."

"*Bano*," he said to the guy holding me, gesturing down a hallway.

The guy grunted and led me down the hall to a door with a women's bathroom sign on it. He opened the door and pushed me inside. "Hurry."

The door shut behind me, and I quickly looked for an escape. Unfortunately, there was only the one door and no windows. And the only vent was way too small for me to try to fit through.

Begrudgingly, I put on the dirty clothes I'd been given over my bathing suit. The T-shirt was too big, but the shorts fit, and I was thankful I had more than a towel covering me.

A loud knock startled me, making me jump. "*Andale!*"

"Jesus fucking Christ, I'm coming!" I yelled back. When I approached the door, I could hear him muttering under his breath in Spanish, so I figured he was right outside the door.

This could be my only chance to get away.

I knew most of the other men had already jumped down in the hole. If I could knock this guy down, I could make a run for the front door and hope that Ford was somewhere nearby. If he wasn't, then I wasn't sure what I would do, but I had to take the chance.

I threw open the door, hitting the man and knocking him to the ground. I took off as fast as my bare feet would take me, running down the hall as the man yelled out in Spanish.

I turned the corner to go to the front of the store, the exit door in sight as the man who'd given me my current outfit stepped out from one of the aisles and clotheslined me.

I fell to the ground hard, the wind knocked out of me as I reached for my neck and gasped for breath. I winced in pain as the man stood over me, sneering down at me. "*Pendeja.*"

I was hauled up a few seconds later, and my original captor gripped me by the arm again, leading me back to the hole in the ground. "In," he said.

When I looked down in the hole, I saw that it led to a tunnel.

Great. I'm being smuggled illegally into Mexico.

I hopped down, and the man followed me. Matteo's cronies led me through the man-made tunnel, and I couldn't believe what was happening. I'd heard Matteo talk about their tunnels and smuggling drugs and people using them, but I definitely never expected to experience it myself.

I rubbed at my sore throat as we walked through the dimly lit passageway, which smelled like mold and dirt. I was glad I wasn't claustrophobic because the enclosed space was narrow and tight, maybe wide enough for a person and a half.

I'm not sure how long we walked for, but it felt like hours. I'd left my phone in the VIP area when the girls and I had gone in the pool, so I had no idea what time it was or how long I'd been gone.

I wondered if my friends were searching for me. I hoped that one of Ford's guys had told them what was going on so that they didn't stay in Vegas looking for me or try to get the cops involved. That would be bad news for Ford, and the cops couldn't do anything once I was in Mexico.

When we finally emerged from the end of the tunnel, another group of men was waiting for us with two SUVs. I was forced in the back of one as they conversed in Spanish again.

I rolled my eyes, exasperated. A few minutes passed before all the men finally loaded up, and we drove off.

I startled awake when the SUV made an abrupt stop. It took me a few moments to register where I was, and I almost cried when I realized the whole thing hadn't been some nightmare.

But I needed to say strong. Matteo enjoyed breaking me, and I wasn't going to give him the satisfaction. Inhaling deeply, I steeled myself for what was to come as the back of the SUV opened, and I was ushered out.

A huge mansion stood before me. I couldn't see anything else but desert and some trees in any direction, and I wondered how far we were from the border.

I sent a silent prayer to Ford. *Please find me.*

I was escorted inside the lavish mansion, which looked like something from Beverly Hills had been transplanted into the middle of a Mexican desert.

The marble floors beneath my dirty feet were cold, and I wanted to scoff at the audacity of the rich interior. A smirk curved my lips as I thought about how my presence would be a blight to Matteo in the perfect world he'd built for himself.

Speaking of the devil himself, Matteo appeared at the top of the extravagant, winding staircase. "Ah, you've finally made it, *hermosa.*"

My lip curled up at his nickname for me. The only nickname I wanted to hear was kitten, and a pang of sadness filled me as I thought about never hearing Ford say it again.

Be strong. He's coming for you.

Matteo walked down the stairs and stood before me, eyeing me up and down with a look of disgust. He started rapidly speaking in Spanish, his tone angry and loud. I only knew some cuss words in the language, and he'd used every one. He was obviously upset about the condition I was brought in.

He snapped his fingers, and two Hispanic women rushed over from a neighboring room. After speaking to them in Spanish, he directed his attention to me, his lips curving up in what I used to think was a charming grin. "I'm sorry for the lack of consideration on my men's part. Luisa and Magda will help you get cleaned up, then we will have a proper reunion."

The thought of a proper reunion with him made me want to throw up. "Fuck you, Matteo," I said before spitting in his face.

I knew from experience that spitting in his face royally pissed him off, and that I'd be punished for it, yet at the moment, I didn't care. I hated him for everything he'd done to me and having me kidnapped at gunpoint was the last straw.

His nostrils flared as he took a handkerchief from his suit pocket and wiped his face, then he backhanded me so hard that I saw stars. "Looks like you will need a little lesson in respect, also."

He started yelling at the two women in Spanish again, and they quickly rushed to my side and escorted me up the stairs. They led me to an opulent bathroom that was bigger than Nina's whole apartment.

After closing the door behind us, one of the women led me to a sitting chair as the other turned on the water in an ivory clawfoot tub. She poured various oils into the running water as we waited for the tub to fill.

Once the tub was full, Luisa and Magda helped me undress and urged me into the bath. I couldn't deny that the water felt amazing, but I'd rather be put in a tub of shit if it meant I was out of Matteo's grasp.

Luisa and Magda wanted to bathe me, but I insisted on washing myself. Once I was finished, they wrapped me in a towel and led me to an adjoining bedroom, which had a luxurious canopy bed with lace and gold accents.

They gave me a long, cream-colored dress that reminded of something Greek goddesses were usually depicted wearing. Then they blow-dried and curled my hair and did my makeup, which I thought was overkill, but Matteo had ridiculous standards. He expected the best and was like a petulant child when he didn't get it.

Once Luisa and Magda were finished, they escorted me back downstairs to the dining room, which had a large glass table with enough seating for twelve. Matteo was sitting at the head of the table, his hair slicked back and wearing a pressed gray suit.

"Ah, that's much better," he commented as Magda and Luisa led me to a chair directly on the left side of Matteo. "*Gracias,*" he thanked dismissively, waving the women away after I'd been seated.

I stared at Matteo with contempt as he smiled at me. "You must be starving. I've had my chef prepare a delicious meal for us tonight."

"I'd rather starve," I replied with a sneer even though my stomach growled with hunger.

He let out an exasperated sigh, like a parent annoyed with their disobedient child. "Why must you make things difficult, *hermosa*? This is what you wanted, isn't?" He gestured around the room. "Luxury and riches."

I crossed my arms over my chest. "Not if I have to share it with you."

He clucked his tongue in disapproval. "Fine." He snapped his fingers, and Luisa and Magda came back in. "If you don't want to cooperate then you can stay in your room."

Fine with me.

Luisa and Magda took me back to the bedroom upstairs and locked me in. I looked for ways out, but the windows had bars and all the entrances were locked.

I flopped down on the bed with a sigh. My face hurt from Matteo's backhand, and I was exhausted. Since there was nothing else to do, I decided to sleep. I wanted to be ready when Ford came for me because I didn't want to think of the alternative.

I awoke to the sounds of shouting and gunfire. *Ford.*

Springing off the bed, I ran to the window and looked out. Night had fallen, and in the darkness, I could see the flash of guns as they were fired.

I have to get out of here.

I ran to the door and tried the handle, hoping in the commotion that Magda or Luisa might've unlocked it so I could get out. It jiggled but wouldn't open. *Dammit.*

I took a few steps back and charged at the door, throwing my shoulder into it to try to bust it open. All I succeeded in was jamming my shoulder.

I paced impatiently in front of the door, trying to figure out a plan. Several minutes passed when I heard the sound of footsteps and voices nearing the door.

A few seconds later, the door flew open, and Matteo stormed in with six men. His face was a mask of rage as he stalked over to me, roughly grabbing me by the bicep. He barked at his men in Spanish as he practically dragged me out of the room.

Knowing that Ford was on the property, I struggled to get out of Matteo's hold. He tightened his grasp as he ushered me down the stairs, surrounded by his men.

Blood and broken glass littered the pristine marble floor of the foyer. The front door was open, and I could see several bodies from both the cartel and MC lying motionless on the front lawn.

Please don't be Ford, please don't be Ford.

My eyes frantically scanned for Ford, but I didn't catch sight of him as Matteo rushed me through the house to the back door. Chaos greeted us when we went outside, the cartel trying to hold off the bikers who'd come to my rescue.

The men guarding Matteo were slowly picked off as we made

our way across the lawn toward a helicopter. *Shit. I can't let him get me in there, or I'll never see Ford again.*

I made myself go limp, dropping to the ground. Matteo cursed as he tried to pick me back up, but I kicked and screamed, making it as difficult as possible for him.

Then he hit me in the face with his gun, and everything went black.

CHAPTER 20

FORD

When we finally made it to the trees bordering Matteo's property, I was about to come undone. Adrenaline rushed through my veins, my heart pounding like it always did before I was about to shed blood. I needed to have Dixyn back in my arms where she belonged.

All my men and the men of the Forsaken readied up, making sure our clips were full and guns were loaded. Apache even had a fucking RPG, which I hated to admit was badass. I had a double shoulder holster with my two X9s, my semi-auto shotgun, an MP5, and a Glock on each hip.

After everyone was locked and loaded, Hawk and my best sniper, AK, got in position to take out Matteo's men manning the guard towers. Both were precise and swift, taking out each of their marks in less than ten seconds.

"Let's move," I motioned, emerging from the cluster of trees.

I kept my eyes on the property, looking for movement or any indication we'd been discovered, but everything seemed normal. The Kings and I were coming up on the back end of the property while the Forsaken were taking the front. While our men took out Matteo's, Apache and I planned to meet in the house and search for Dixyn.

I wanted to charge in there with guns blazing, but using stealth and surprise was the best option, considering the situation, and we needed to use that to our advantage for as long as we could.

Matteo's property was enclosed by a stone wall which we'd either have to blow up or jump because there was no gate. AK had some grenades that would do the trick, but that would definitely alert everyone to our presence.

But when an alarm went off, and gunfire sounded from the front of the property, that didn't matter anymore. "Light it up, AK," I instructed my sergeant at arms.

He tossed two grenades at the wall, and we backed up out of the range of the explosion. When the smoke cleared, there was a nice sized opening in the wall for us to enter through.

"Bring 'em hell, boys!" I yelled as I charged through.

Matteo's men were making their way toward the front of the property, drawn by the Forsaken since they'd obviously been discovered first. I quickly scanned for Dixyn before letting my MP5 sing, taking out several of Matteo's men.

My men spread out as headed for the house, my main focus on finding Dixyn. She had to be inside somewhere; otherwise, Apache would've signaled me that he'd found her.

As I made a beeline for the back door, a group of cartel lackeys came running out. Every minute that ticked by made me more enraged, and each man who got in my way was going to feel my wrath.

I lit them up, but two were able to take cover before I took them out. They shot at me, so I had to duck behind a ridiculous fountain for cover.

"You okay, Pres?" AK called out as he shot at a few men from behind a tree.

"I'd be better once I get in there and rescue my lady," I said as I peeked around the fountain. A couple of bullets whizzed by my head as others embedded in the stone of the fountain.

He laughed as he put a bullet between the eyes of one of Matteo's men. AK reveled in destruction and mayhem, so I was sure he was loving every minute of the bloodshed. That was one of the reasons I'd made him my sergeant at arms. He definitely knew his way around weapons. "I can cover you," he shouted.

Before I could respond, I heard Dixyn's screams. My head snapped in the direction of the piercing sound, and my blood boiled when I saw Matteo knock Dixyn out with his gun. I was going to kill that motherfucker. "Dixyn!" I let out in a howl of rage.

Matteo's head jerked up toward me as he slung Dixyn over his shoulder, and he winked at me.

And I lost it.

Charging from behind the fountain, I took out the remaining two men guarding Matteo, then chased after him. I couldn't let him get Dixyn on that chopper or I'd probably never see her again.

The blades of the helicopter started turning, and I cursed, fearing I wouldn't reach them in time. Then I saw Apache in the distance with the RPG aimed at the chopper and stopped.

He fired and hit his target. The helicopter exploded in a blast of orange and yellow, shrapnel flying everywhere. Matteo and Dixyn were thrown backward from the blast, landing about ten feet from where they were.

"Dixyn!" I yelled as I ran toward them, concerned about her being injured from the blast.

Matteo scrambled to get up, frantically darting his eyes around. I followed his gaze. The Kings and Forsaken had taken out most of his men and were taking care of the rest.

"Nowhere else to run," I remarked, slowing my pace as I reached him.

Apache came up from behind, chuckling. "Sorry about your chopper."

Matteo picked Dixyn up, and she wobbled unsteadily on her feet as he placed a gun against her head. She was obviously dazed, eyes blinking several times as her brows furrowed in confusion.

My heart was about to bust out of my chest. "Let her go," I demanded, pointing my X9 at him.

Matteo sneered, pressing his gun harder against Dixyn's temple. Her chest started heaving with heavy breaths, and her eyes widened as she finally realized what was going on. "Ford," she whimpered.

Tears started streaming down her face, and my gut twisted with guilt and fear.

"You're not in any place to making demands, *puto*. This bitch is mine, and I can do whatever I want with her," Matteo snapped.

Apache rounded on Matteo, shouting in anger, "My daughter ain't nobody's bitch!" He cocked his gun, aiming it at Matteo as he came next to me. "I'd listen to Bullet if I were you. You're outnumbered, and we ain't leaving without her."

Matteo chuckled, keeping Dixyn strategically in front of him like a shield. "If you want her, you're going to have to pry her from my cold, dead hands. And if I'm going down, I'm taking her with me. If I can't have her, nobody will." He locked his eyes on mine. "Including you."

Rage was boiling in my veins, and I was doing my best to keep myself under control even though I wanted to empty my clip into the motherfucker's skull.

I glanced at Apache. We'd talked about what would happen in a situation like the one we were in. Dixyn wouldn't like it, but we were backed into a corner. He gave me a silent nod.

Taking a deep breath, I readied myself. Apache started talking shit and took a step toward Matteo, who instinctively aimed at him. "Don't," he warned.

As soon as he moved the gun from her head, Apache and I both rushed him. Matteo shot at Apache first, then at me. "Dixyn, move!" I shouted as I approached.

In all the commotion, she was able to wrench herself from Matteo's grasp right before I collided with him. I tackled him to the ground, one hand on his gun and the other around his throat.

Matteo was a dangerous man, but I was bigger and had more motivation. I had at least fifty pounds on him. Plus, he usually had others do his dirty work for him, so I was pretty sure I had more experience fighting and inflicting damage than he did.

Anger and adrenaline raced through me as I pried the gun from his hand and hit him in the face with the butt of it, just as he had to Dixyn. Tossing the gun, I tightened my grip on his throat as I rained down punches with my free fist. He struggled beneath me, pounding at my arms to let him go.

Killing him would have consequences with the cartel, but I didn't care. I wasn't going to give him the opportunity to hurt Dixyn ever again.

Once his face was a bloody pulp and his struggle weakened, I took my knife out. "See you in hell, *puto.*"

Then I slit his throat. His blood poured out as he reached for his wound. After cleaning his blood off my knife with his shirt, I stood, and Dixyn immediately ran over to me. "You came for me," she sobbed.

"Of course I did." Taking her in my arms, I buried my face in her hair and inhaled her sweet scent. She clung to me for dear life, crying into my chest. "It's okay, baby. It's all over now. He'll never hurt you again."

Then she surprised me by taking my knife, screaming as she plunged it over and over into Matteo's chest. He was already almost dead from my wound, but she obviously didn't care.

I stopped counting after fifteen stabs, letting Dixyn get all her anger and pain out. I knew what it was like to seek retribution and finally get revenge, having done it several times with my mom's exes once I'd become a man.

She was sobbing again by the time she finished, slumping to her knees and letting my knife fall to the ground. She was covered in Matteo's blood, but I still picked her up and held her tight.

Dixyn didn't calm down for several minutes. My heart rate finally started to slow down as I held her, and I released a sigh of relief that she was back in my arms where she belonged.

Then, the pain came. The adrenaline flowing through me was wearing off, and I was starting to feel my injuries. I knew I'd taken a couple of bullets but didn't know where or how many.

I grunted as Dixyn pulled away, wiping her face. We both looked down and saw the bullet holes. Dixyn gasped. "Oh shit. You got hit."

There were bullet wounds in my shoulder, forearm, and beneath my ribs. Since I was still standing, I didn't think anything vital had been hit.

Some of my men ran over to us. "You okay, Pres?" Dead Man asked. "Y'all look like hell."

"Just a couple of bullets. I'll live."

Dixyn looked up at me with fear. "We need to call an ambulance."

Dead Man, AK, and Cowboy laughed. "Can we keep her, boss?" AK joked.

I chuckled. "We're in Mexico, kitten. I'm not getting anything done here. And I don't do hospitals."

She frowned. "Don't be stubborn, Ford. You've been shot."

I winced as I draped my arm around her. "Ain't the first time and probably won't be the last time."

"Is that your blood?" Dead Man asked Dixyn, looking her up and down. Her light-colored dress was almost completely red, and her face and arms were splattered with the bodily fluid, also.

"No. It's his," she gestured at Matteo's lifeless body, frowning. Then she spat on it.

"We're definitely keeping her," AK commented with a laugh.

I looked down at her and smiled. "Yeah, I think I'll keep her."

Apache came over with Raleigh and Jameson. They were covered in blood and dirt, and Apache had taken a few bullets, as well. "You okay, Dixie girl?" Apache asked, leaning on Jameson.

Dixyn looked at her family, her eyes widening as she noticed they were all there for the first time. "How did you ...?" she trailed off in confusion, brows furrowing.

A lopsided grin tipped Apache's lips as he nodded toward me. "Bullet here came for reinforcements."

Dixyn darted her eyes to me, then back to her father. "And you came?" Her voice cracked.

Apache's grin fell, and he frowned. "Of course, baby girl."

Dixyn hesitated a few seconds before rushing over to her family, and they all enveloped her in a group hug.

I couldn't help but smile. I'd felt like shit since causing the rift between them, even if it had brought us closer together.

When they pulled apart, Dixyn came back to me and helped hold me up again. I held her tight against my side, not wanting to ever let her go.

As if I didn't have enough surprises that day, Apache limped over to me and extended his hand. "Thank you for saving my little girl."

Blinking in shock, I slowly took his hand and shook it. "Thanks for having our backs."

Apache nodded. "We're gonna head back. See you on the other side."

Dixyn said her goodbyes to her family as I talked with the guys. "Any baggage we need to deal with?" I asked.

"Nope," AK said. "Kojack, Hook, and Ajax are tying up loose ends."

"Good. Did we lose anyone?"

Cowboy's face hardened as he nodded. "We lost Deuce. A couple Forsaken, too."

"Fuck," I cursed. "Make sure we get his body. We ain't leaving it here to rot with these wetbacks."

Dixyn came back over to me, which immediately brightened my mood. "Hey, kitten."

"Hey." She frowned as her eyes darted between my wounds. "You really should see a doctor."

I scoffed. "I'll be fine, babe. Don't worry."

"Well, at least let me have Meghan look at you. She's a nurse."

I smiled down at her. "I love you."

Her head whipped up toward me, her gaze meeting mine. She stared at me for several seconds, tears in her eyes. "You mean it?"

I tucked a strand of her wild hair behind her ear. She was a fucking mess, covered in blood and dirt, and it made me love her even more. "Yeah, kitten, I do."

Eyes watering, she smiled. "I love you, too, old man."

I chuckled, happier than I'd ever been even with three bullets in me. I draped my arm around her shoulders. "Let's go home."

EPILOGUE

Dixyn

I f you would have told me a few months ago that I'd be sitting at a biker barbecue with my family and the Suicide Kings, I would've told you to stay on your meds.

As I sat in Ford's lap while he laughed at some dirty joke my dad made, I almost pinched myself. I never would've believed that I would be where I was, but to be honest, I couldn't be happier. I'd been accepted into the community college in Laughlin, and couldn't wait to start school.

My life had completely changed, and I felt like I was on top of the world.

After the Kings and Forsaken came together to save me, my dad and Ford put their bullshit behind them and called a truce. Two weeks later, we were all having a barbecue at Ford's shop.

I laughed as I took it all in. I couldn't believe what had happened since my grandpa died, and I wondered what he would make of the whole situation. He'd probably get a kick out of it.

There was still some tension between some of the guys on each side, but my dad and Ford made sure to nip any bullshit in the bud before anything got out of hand. Ford putting his life on the line and taking three bullets for me really changed my dad's opinion of him, and he wasn't going to let any of his men give him or the Kings any shit.

I let out a sigh of contentment. I was relieved we didn't have to sneak around anymore. Especially with the news I had to tell Ford.

I pulled him into his office, closing the door behind us. He had me pressed against the door, lips on mine before the lock had even clicked shut.

"I've been thinking about those lips all night," he growled, kissing me deeper. "And that tight pussy around me."

I giggled, trying to control the building desire within me. I pushed back against him so I could talk. "I need to tell you something."

Ford frowned down at me in concern. "What's up? Is everything okay?"

I forced a nervous smile. I was afraid of how he would react to what I was about to tell him. We'd been through so much the past couple of months. "Yeah, everything's great."

He arched a brow at me, a nervous grin tugging at the corner of his mouth. "What is it, kitten?"

I took his hand and placed it on my stomach. "You're gonna be a dad, old man."

He glanced down at our joined hands on my stomach, then back up at me, eyes alight with both excitement and confusion. "You're pregnant?"

I nodded, reminiscing back to the night on Spirit Mountain. Based on the timing, that was when I suspected Ford had gotten me pregnant. He really had claimed me. "I took a test last night. And another this morning. They were both positive."

He let out a whoop of joy as he picked me up and twirled me around. I hadn't expected him to react the way he was, so I was relieved to say the least.

Setting me down, he planted a kiss on my lips. His happiness was evident in the brightness in his dark eyes and ear-to-ear grin on his face.

"You're not mad?" I asked, shocked by his reaction.

"Mad? Why would I be mad?" He tucked my hair behind my ear and looked deep in my eyes. "My old lady's gonna give me a baby."

I smiled. He'd been so against being tied down so I didn't think he'd be happy that I was pregnant. I actually feared he would make me get an abortion. "I love you."

He kissed me again. "And I love you, kitten. You've made me a very happy man."

I didn't know what the future held for us, but I knew it would be an exciting ride with Ford by my side. And I couldn't wait to see where the road took us.

THE END

ACKNOWLEDGMENTS

This story is different from anything I've written before, and I was nervous about taking on this genre because I feel there are certain expectations with MC novels. I loved writing Ford and Dixyn's story and hope I did the genre justice.

I was inspired by my boyfriend's grandfather's funeral. He was a biker and when we attended his funeral, I was blown away by the number of bikers from different clubs that showed up to pay their respects. It was a humbling experience to say the least, and I really wanted to capture that with this story. I hope you enjoyed reading it as much as I enjoyed writing it.

In memory of Elvin "Corky" Bethel
October 26, 1945 to March 4, 2015

OTHER BOOKS BY NIKKI SPARXX

What We Left Behind

The Scars Series

The Scars of Us

Mending Scars

The Scars Duet

The Scars of Him

The Platinum Hotel Series

Meet Me in Room 108 (Available in KU)

The Elemental Prophecy Series

Envisioned (Available in KU)

Emblazed

Empowered

Connect with Nikki:

www.facebook.com/NikkiSparxxAuthor

www.nikkisparxx.wordpress.com

Made in the USA
Monee, IL
05 May 2023

32926793R00125